The Cut Throat

(A Carmel McAlistair Mystery)

by

Liz Graham

For information, email **Cozy Cat Press**, cozycatpress@aol.com or visit our website at: www.cozycatpress.com

COZY CAT PRESS

ISBN: 978-1-946063-10-6

Printed in the United States of America

Cover design by Paula Ellenberger
www.paulaellenberger.com

1 2 3 4 5 6 7 8 9 10

Thanks to editors Joanne and Iona, without whom these books would not have happened. And also to Kathryn, Bev and Christine, who believed in me!

Chapter 1

Ruscan Milanovic was gone. She wasn't sure, but suspected she had misplaced him.

Now in this cottage on the other side of the world, back on her home island in a tiny cove that no one had ever heard of and where she knew nobody, Carmel McAlistair could bury herself in her writing. A dramatic reaction to the pain of loss, no doubt, but it made sense. She would be a hermit now, dedicating herself to a solitary life where she could do no more damage.

It wasn't that she was hiding. No, but he wouldn't find her here, even if he wanted to. Even if he wasn't dead. And nothing was certain, that was the only fact she knew.

Ruscan would have argued the point, of course. He, the Ukranian-born, self-made millionaire whose English was more perfect than her own. Ruscan who couldn't stand to have anything out of place, was now out of place himself. It might have been her doing but some things were better left unthought.

St. Jude Without had found her and become the setting of her latest reincarnation. She liked the way the mountain behind her crouched over the sparse houses, nestling the tiny outpost in its stony embrace and shielding it from the probing fingers of the morning sun. A single road snaked southward around its knee, the gravelled surface the only tenuous connection to the modern world outside—unless, of course, one was prepared to brave the ocean and that rickety wharf.

On this warm late August afternoon, a woman down on the point hung her laundry to catch the fresh sea breeze, and a black dog snuffled the roadside scrub for the day's idle gossip. It could be a place of innocence, at first glance. A clean place. Not like the smog-laden skies of Taipei which had swallowed her lover. Who knew someone could vanish in mid-air?

This was the perfect seclusion demanded by her 'herm-attitude.' If that was a word.

"Herm-attitude," she said aloud, using the sound of her own voice to block the thoughts revolving round inside her head. She removed the white wine from the fridge. Looking through the out-dated cupboards in the kitchen, the first vessel to hand was a jam jar. Carmel shrugged and proceeded to pour. One good thing about being a hermit was that you could be as eccentric as you liked.

The fridge kicked in with a rattle and a jump, so she hip-checked the door shut, grimacing as she noticed an old mirror in a cheap plastic frame, krazy-glued onto the door many years ago. She pried at an edge with her free pinky, but it wasn't coming off. Her own blue eyes looked back at her from the spotted glass, the wide mouth below serious, the nose long. And another wrinkle starting on her forehead.

Carmel brought both bottle and jam-jar out onto the front veranda overlooking the point of land and the water beyond as she contemplated her new life alone. Although there were many she called friends scattered throughout the world, Carmel had never been one for close relationships. Just the once. And she'd lost him. She considered herself an island of sorts.

He had happened—the love of her life—right when she was ready for him. She left her high-flying friends to be with him in domesticity and it had worked out pretty well. She'd thought. But he had disappeared so suddenly, leaving a hole in her heart as large as Taiwan. Older, wiser and not quite broke, she'd headed back to the island she'd started from for a new beginning, to see if she could get it right this time.

"What is it about islands?" she asked a passing seagull, then settled back on the veranda with her drink, watching the ferry chugging across the Tickle to the land mass sheering out of the surrounding sea. "They're often hard to reach, perhaps isolated, sometimes out in the middle of unprotected seas.... Each island has its own mystique."

"They say no man is an island, but I think people are," Carmel argued out loud as if Ruscan were there to refute her words. "People are like islands in that all of us are isolated within the sea of humanity. Each person has their own mystery, too." She sat back, satisfied that she had won that round, and thinking that would be a good lead into the next article.

Or perhaps she was just spending too much time with herself.

A niggling insecurity deep within suspected that she had done something to chase Ruscan away. Okay, so it hadn't all been roses and sunshine. He liked order, and would get a bit put out with her clutter and disorganization. They'd had some lovely all-out arguments about politics and food choices and how to load the dishwasher. She giggled aloud at the memory.

No matter the situation, life somehow works out for the optimist. Once Carmel was back on her native soil, this house had fallen into her lap as if by magic. An affordable ocean-side rental but close to the city in her price range? The real estate agent was already laughing as he flicked through the property sheets, the negative answer on his lips, when his attention was arrested by this house. He swore he hadn't seen this listing before, he who knew all the houses available through his office.

And who had ever heard of St. Jude Without? Despite its proximity to the city where she'd spent her formative years, she hadn't known it existed and even he had to look it up on the map. But there it was, the price was right and she got the key the same afternoon.

Carmel sighed and took a long sip, the afternoon sun warm on her legs as she gazed westward. There was enough money in her savings to live modestly in this small oddly-shaped rented cottage outside the city, in the forgotten cove of St. Jude Without at the end of the long pot-holed road which hugged the cliff's edge of the North Point Road. The house itself was perhaps two hundred years old, situated at a 45 degree angle to the road. Maybe that had inspired Mr. Ryan, her new landlord, to create a round veranda overlooking the road and water, from which practically the whole community was visible.

The house was not attractive and lacked all curb appeal, which could account for its affordability. A squat stone and clapboard structure, it looked like no other house she'd ever seen. The interior hadn't been touched since the 1980's, and would have been called retro if its renovator had had a smidgeon of taste. But, alas, he didn't, and neither did his wife. This lady had since passed on to the big bay in the sky and her husband, Mr. Ryan, to the state of Florida, taking advantage of a cheap beachside condo in St. Pete's where he'd never have to do another renovation or decorating project again.

"Still, I don't have to look at it," she reminded herself. "But I have a view of the water, woods and wilderness behind me. With this wide expanse before me, I never have to feel claustrophobic again." She lifted her jam jar in a toast.

Slowly, she became aware of being the subject of intense scrutiny. A woman with flowing red hair stood watchfully on the porch of the bungalow across the road, hardly visible at all among the shadows of the lowering sun behind her house. She wore a simple purple Indian cotton dress, the kind in style for hippies over the past fifty years. Once eye contact had been established between the two, the woman made her purposeful bare-foot way towards her.

"Hi," the redhead called as she made her way up the steps to the deck. She was carrying a plate with slices of carrot cake topped with oodles of cream cheese icing. "You must be Carmel. Uncle Frank told me about you. I'm Bridget."

She stood at the top of the stairs expectantly, one eyebrow cocked, and with her other hand removed a crystal goblet from the voluminous pocket of her dress. As she held it out, it caught the sun, tossing out prisms of sparkle like fairy dust.

"Any more of that bottle left?" she asked Carmel. Both sets of eyes turned to the freshly opened bottle sitting in a ring of condensation on the small pine table.

A tentative alliance grew as the afternoon sun lengthened, nurtured through carrot cake and wine. Bridget looked to be in her late thirties. A potter by trade, she had lived in the city while a child but had taken over her grandmother's tiny house in the cove after the passing of that much loved lady.

"I pretty much grew up out here," Bridget said. "I came out to see Nan every chance I could get, even in high school."

"Not much out here for a kid to do, surely," Carmel replied, confessing the restlessness of her own teenage years. She'd grown up in the city, and even then she couldn't wait to get out into the 'real' world. Perhaps it had been the confines of the convent she'd wanted to shake off.

It was revealed that, unlike herself, Bridget had never travelled further than Halifax. "But why?" the redhead asked her back in reply, a blank look on her face. "Why would I ever want to leave here?"

This question stumped her for a moment, for far too many answers flooded into the space it opened. "Well, there's Paris, for one thing," Carmel said. "Paris and… and Stockholm! The Mona Lisa, and, oh, all the fabulous artwork in Europe, and the Great Wall of China, the Crystal Caves in Bermuda, the rock palaces of Petra…" This could go on for a while, she realized, and she was running out of fingers on which to count. "How can you even ask? The whole world is out there. Don't you want to see it all?"

"This is my home."

"Yes, St. Jude Without is your home, I understand that," Carmel said. "And it's a gorgeous spot. But you can leave and come back. There's so much to learn out there."

"I can't leave the cove," the other said, shaking her head. "Not now, too late for that."

"Your uncle Frank did," Carmel reminded her. "He's moved to Florida."

"Yeah, but he's not from here," Bridget said. "He was born in Bauline, up the shore. He doesn't have the cove in his blood."

"You mean the cove won't let you leave?" She was joking of course when she asked.

"Don't laugh. The cove found you, didn't it?"

Carmel stopped laughing. Bridget could be right, in a way. The real estate agent hadn't known about this listing, yet it had appeared when Carmel did… But this was nonsense. She put down her jar of wine. She'd had enough.

"Y'see, someone's got to keep an eye on things." Bridget sat motionless, watching two gulls playing in the wind, riding the current as it took them in from the sea. "My world is here," she said, turning to Carmel. "The cove needs me." The lowering sun caught golden glints within the green depths of her eyes. "My family, my history. I know everything about this place." She pointed to the birds. "For example, you see that gull there, to the left? The one with the black bit on his tail? We nursed his grandmother when she hurt her wing. That was a few years back. His father used to come right to my back door—he liked fried scrunchions the best. He disappeared; I think he might have died of clogged arteries." She paused as if in reflection. "Did you know gulls stay with one partner for life?"

Carmel wasn't sure if the other woman was pulling her leg, but Bridget hadn't yet shown much of a sense of humour. All this information about a single gull family, when there were millions—no, probably billions of seagulls in the world. She found it a little weird and—yes, creepy even—the way this young woman talked about the cove as if it had a physical presence.

"How can you tell it's the same bird?" she asked. "They all look alike to me."

"Our families have shared the cove together for over two hundred years. You get to know them. Besides, there's not a lot else to do around here. There's always time, here."

Time. Until Ruscan, Carmel would find herself getting antsy after spending only six months in a place. When that happened, another great new idea would hit her and she'd be off into the sunset. What she couldn't see was that her life had been a series of great new starts. Being of an impetuous and imaginative nature, she would dive headlong into new pursuits with the certainty of finally finding the one thing that would make her happy, or would at least fulfill her. That is, until she got bored or disillusioned or distracted by something shiny. Or fell flat on her face, like this time.

"My great-great-great—I don't know how many more—great grandfather settled this cove and built your house around 1800." Bridget was informing her as she leaned back into her chair and closed her eyes to bask in the late afternoon sun. "He retired from pirating and settled here in the cove."

Carmel squinted doubtfully over to her friend. "I thought pirates were a bit earlier, say, in the 1600's," she said. "Peter Easton and that crowd? The golden age of pirates ended in 1625."

Bridget shrugged without opening her eyes. "That's the story. They say Jeremiah was a pirate, down off Bermuda. There's a portrait of him somewhere; he liked to dress up in the old-fashioned pirate garb. He got out of the business after he'd made enough money, but that didn't help him any," she said. "The local priest objected to his presence, turned him into the authorities, and then built the church right next door just for spite."

"What happened to him? Jeremiah, I mean," Carmel asked.

"Hanged," Bridget replied. "His body was tarred and left to rot on Gibbet Hill, overlooking the city."

"Oh," said Carmel, momentarily at a loss for words. "Sorry about that. I mean, him being your ancestor and all."

Bridget sat up to look at her with her clear gaze. "He didn't mind overly, I think," she said. "That's what happened back then. You became a pirate to get rich, but you knew there would be a payback coming up. What pissed him off was the priest ratting on him like that, after he'd gotten out of the business."

"Ah," said Carmel, pretending she understood, although she didn't. "Well, at least if he was hung in the city, he won't be haunting the house," she joked.

"Hmm," Bridget replied, her eyes sliding away. She pointed to a huge stump to the left of them. "Actually, he was hung on that tree there." A full three feet across its middle, each ring so thin it was barely discernable around the rotted center hole, this was perhaps the last remainder of the ancient pines which once covered the whole island. "Uncle Frank had to cut it down after the last big hurricane."

Carmel sat back, appalled at this close proximity to historical horrors. It was okay to read about these things in a book, or to visit ancient ruins and hear the stories of violent death that had happened in these sorts of places, but to be sitting not ten feet away from the spot where this woman's own ancestor had been tried, sentenced and lynched by a vigilante mob made it— well—a little too close for comfort.

"They took his body and hung it on the hill over the city as a warning for others not to go at the pirating," her new acquaintance continued, then just as casually hopped back to another subject. "Would it bother you? A ghost, I mean."

This was firmer ground, the black and white of possible and impossible. "They might if they existed," Carmel said, smiling. "But ghosts aren't real, they're made-up stories to frighten children into behaving, like fairies and darbies and magic." She was an expert on these things, having been told in explicit detail by Sister Mary Oliphant the nasty punishments awaiting naughty children when she was herself a young girl.

"Magic," Bridget said, seizing on the last word. Her creamy skin glowed in the last of the sun's rays and Carmel realized that beneath the masses of hennaed hair, Bridget must be a natural redhead. Her neighbour lowered her voice and leaned closer. "Do you believe in magic?"

Carmel crossed her legs away from the other woman and withdrew in her chair, just a fraction. "Harry Potter and wizards and that sort of stuff?" Carmel asked. "No. Really, no."

"Never felt the presence of spirits? Of things beyond this world?"

Bridget was studying her with an uncomfortable intensity. She had the unsettled feeling that she was being tested in some way. "Never," she stated, meeting the other's gaze head on and deciding to turn the challenge around. "Have you?"

The other shrugged, breaking her scrutiny. "Yeah, there's a lot of weird stuff out there, if you know what you're looking at."

Great. Her first acquaintance in her new home was turning out to be the resident flake. She wondered if there were drugs involved, or if the woman's strangeness just came from spending too long in this cove, away from the twenty-first century which bustled beyond the mountain.

"Here?" Carmel asked. "Do you mean, there's strange stuff here in this cove particularly?"

"Here, too," Bridget replied in a matter-of-fact tone as if they were discussing the local flora and fauna. "Anywhere, really. But if you're not sensitive, it wouldn't bother you."

She was having a hard time figuring this woman out. On one hand, the woman looked and spoke like a flippy-hippie New Ager, with her bare feet, Indian cotton dress and talk of spirits. But on the other, she appeared to have her feet firmly rooted in the sparse topsoil of the cove, intimately acquainted with the minutiae of the daily lives of each inhabitant, even the lineage of gulls. Hell, she could probably relate the history of every boulder strewn alongside the gravel road of St. Jude Without. And Bridget wasn't floaty, or at least she didn't cultivate that air of mystery and otherworldliness so commonly found among the self-proclaimed spiritual crowd.

Carmel listened with half an ear as Bridget went on to tell her about the berries to be had up the 'hill,' as she called the looming mountain behind them, and she finally put her finger on it. There was no bull with Bridget. She was what she was and that's all there was to it. And as far as Bridget was concerned, you were free to take her or leave her—she wasn't looking to impress. Carmel was undecided as to whether or not she liked the woman, and Bridget probably wouldn't care one way or another. That helped swing the balance in favour of liking her.

She realized with a start that Bridget had changed topics and was asking her a question.

"Sorry, what was that?" she asked. "I sort of got lost in thought there."

"Yeah, you were looking at me pretty hard. Trying to figure me out, were you?" The redhead was grinning at her, with no offense taken. Before Carmel had the opportunity to deny this insight, Bridget glanced down at the road. "Dammit. I have to go."

She disappeared into Carmel's front door in a whirl of purple skirt. The wooden screen door slammed behind her.

"Did I just see Bridget here?" The clipped British accent came from a woman standing on the road, looking up at Carmel. Her short hair was cut in a thick fringe across her forehead and her plain t-shirt showed a sturdy build, while the Capri trekking pants with numerous pockets emphasized her thick ankles. She looked to be about Carmel's own age, early forties.

"She was," Carmel replied, looking at the front door. "She had to go though…"

"Roxanne Henderson," the newcomer said as she mounted the stairs uninvited and shook Carmel's hand. Her eyes seemed friendly enough behind the thick lenses of her glasses. "I'm leasing the cottage at the end of the point." She indicated across the way, where the only side road in the cove meandered down the point of land with houses scattered along its length.

"Lovely location," Carmel said, eyeing the proximity of the ocean to the snug-looking cottage. From up here, it looked like the tiny house was perched right on the small cliff's edge at the end of the meadow. *How wonderful*, she thought, *to be out there during winter gales, hearing the waves crash against the beach.* Stormy weather was the best.

"Yes," the English woman replied shortly, taking the seat just vacated by Bridget. "A little too close to the salt water for my liking. But if I'd known this house was available, it would have been my first choice." She cast a suspicious glance around the veranda, finally coming to rest on Carmel.

Great. Another oddball resident of the strange little cove.

"Are you working here?" Carmel asked the newcomer to change the focus of the conversation.

"Lecturing at the university right now," the other replied. "Anthropology and folklore. So what brings you here?"

"Just back from travelling the world," Carmel said, omitting any reference to her recent heartbreak. "I need a home base from which to write. I'm a travel writer," she added, seeing the question forming in the other's eyes.

"A fellow traveller," Roxanne said. "How delightfully refreshing. So you've nothing to do with what some might call the 'paranormal'?"

"What?" Carmel shook her head. "No. Nothing to do with any other worlds, I assure you."

"You're not here looking for anything?" Roxanne relaxed a little in her chair. "That's alright, then."

"Can I offer you a jar of wine?" Carmel asked, more out of politeness than a desire to encourage the woman's stay.

"No, never touch the stuff." Roxanne waved away the offer, although she seemed quite content to remain. "My body is my temple and all that, don't you know."

Roxanne, despite her refusal of alcohol, became quite chatty and friendly. After discussing their mutual love of travel, the topic of the cove arose, quite naturally.

"Funny, I'd never heard of this cove before moving here," Carmel noted.

"An interesting place name," Roxanne was quick to agree. "St. Jude Without. Of course, I'm familiar with St. Jude, the patron saint of hopeless causes, but one wonders what is it exactly that St. Jude is without?"

"The word 'without' also means 'outside of,' as opposed to 'within'," Carmel informed her. She'd always loved words, and had spent many hours of her solitary childhood reading the ancient Oxford dictionary in the convent library. "It's an old, rare form little used today. Usually occurs at the end of the road, outside of a main community."

"That fits, then," the other replied. "Oh, look at the time," she said, glancing at her watch. "I was looking for Bridget, need to pick her brain about something. If you see her, ask her to drop in, will you?"

"Sure," Carmel said. "If I see her."

"I must be pushing on," Roxanne said as she stood up to go. "I have a 'date' with my landlord."

She smiled in a surprisingly self-deprecatory way, unexpected from this other-wise very confident woman.

"My landlord insisted I be present while he fixes up the plumbing. Not that I can help, I'm sure. I think it's just a ruse to be with me, to tell the truth. He's a very handsome man," she added, giggling like a girl, then blushed again as if this had surprised even herself, and set off down the laneway with a bounce in her step.

Carmel stared after her. Well! He must be quite the male if he could turn the head of this serious, studious woman. She thought back to the men she'd seen so far passing through the cove and shook her head. Definitely couldn't recall seeing anyone she'd call good-looking, but then again, no accounting for tastes, she told herself. And she thanked God that the days of making a fool of herself over a man were long gone. Carmel had reconciled herself to her single state and was quite comfortable there again. She told herself that at least five times a day, so it had to be true.

"She gone?" Bridget came back outside.

"She asked that you drop in."

"Like that'll happen."

They both watched in silence as Roxanne made her sturdy way down the gravelled lane. Clouds drifted over the westering sun, chilling the atmosphere.

"She's really not his type," muttered Bridget, an unexpected frown creasing her brow, still watching the slight figure dance down the distant road. Seeing Carmel's perplexed glance, Bridget rolled her eyes. "Really."

With that, the redhead slipped down the steps, carelessly leaving her crystal glass behind, before Carmel had a chance to question her about the tension between her and the English woman.

Carmel battered the fish she'd bought earlier at the big box grocery store at the outskirts of the city. A simple pan fry for supper, to test the efficiency of the burners of the old stove which came with the house. Although the white enamel of the appliance was a little chipped in spots from obvious hard use over the years, it would serve her well enough.

She sniffed the aroma from the hot pan—sole in a browned butter sauce. She'd forgotten to add the salt, but reasoned that as she was using salted butter, well, the two should even themselves out. Shouldn't they?

"Perfect," she said, then opened the window to let the smell of cooking out, as the old kitchen had been designed before over-stove fans became the norm. Few things were worse than the stale smell of fish after the meal was eaten.

A movement darker than the lowering twilight outside caught her attention, and she leaned over to the window to get a better look. Two bright yellow eyes jumped out at her.

She startled back before she realized what she was seeing.

"More company?" she said with a smile as the yellow eyes glanced from her to the pan in her hand. "Well, cat, there may be enough for two, if you mind your manners."

Carmel liked cats, their independent spirit and total selfishness. The nuns had always had one or two around the convent to control the rodent population in the old stone building close to the river. However, the adult Carmel had never stayed in one place long enough and so had never had one of her own. Perhaps that could change now she was settled. The idea appealed to her— the solitary hermit and her cat.

She placed her own plate in the oven to keep warm while she prepared a salad, after cutting a small portion of fish for the visitor. The house had come with a selection of mismatched china saucers poked away in the cupboard and some old books on a shelf in the living room which she had yet to examine. She removed a particularly pretty saucer embellished with deep red roses. Opening the back door, she laid the dish of mashed sole at a distance from her on the step.

The cat paused on the window sill, allowing Carmel to get a good look and, in turn, sizing her up. A tuxedo cat, black and white, with just a scrape of white on his nose. She was pretty sure it was a 'he' at any rate, with its large head and brawny shoulders.

"It's all yours," she said. The smell of the fish must have overpowered any reservations he had about this new human, for he lightly leaped down to land exactly in front of the dish. With one eye alert for any sudden movements, he inhaled the fish, then sat back to lick the last morsels off his lips.

"You don't look like you're starving," Carmel mused as she realized for the first time the size of the creature. A sleek coat covered a round and smooth body, almost sausage-like in his fullness. "My God, you're huge!"

As if grinning with delight at his own beauty, the cat's lower tooth hooked its upper lip, and she noticed in the light from the open door he was missing half an ear. She laughed out loud at the ridiculous picture he presented, and he yawned, stretched and turned down the steps, his tail lifted happily and belly swaying as he made off purposefully into the darkness.

She crossed her arms and leaned against the doorway, watching him disappear into the night.

A flickering of lights from the woods behind the back yard caught her eye, light laughter and a drift of music carried on the light breeze. Kids playing in the old graveyard perhaps. It was all so faint, they must be a long way off, and she wondered how far back the woods went under the looming hill with its bald rock face, invisible now at night. She could go exploring tomorrow, for there were sure to be paths. Perhaps Bridget was right about the cove being a magical place– –especially if by magic you meant a safe place where kids could play out of doors at night with nary a parent hovering in sight in these days of politically correct child rearing.

For the second time that day, she had the sensation of being watched, this time an eerie prickling of the downy hairs along the back of her neck. Were one of the kids close by? She scanned the darkening woods past the overgrown flower beds and bushes, but could see no hint of a person.

If they're hiding as part of the game, I won't give them away, she thought, a small smile forming on her face. She was suddenly happy to be part of this community.

And tomorrow, Bridget had promised to take her berry picking up the hill to a spot she knew. Late August was the time for blueberries, her new friend had assured her, and there were lots to be had on top of the rocky mountain.

Carmel closed the kitchen door, exploring the idea of foraging for her food and living off the land, and finding she liked it, very much. She'd watched a small fishing boat landing on the wharf earlier, so perhaps she could buy local fish freshly caught from the sea. The chef in her delighted at the idea. And surely that was the sound of cows lowing from the farm at the end of the road. Where there were cows, there were milk and butter, and there would almost certainly be chickens and free-run eggs, and vegetables in season. Her mouth watered at the thought.

After her solitary and simple supper, she looked into the old-fashioned parlour at the boxes of her life demanding to be unpacked, and promptly turned her back on the lot of them, appalled at the effort the task would require. The night was too warm to stay inside. Still a little muzzy-headed from her early evening wine with Bridget, she decided to make a cup of tea and indulge in a cigarette on the front veranda. It was a habit which she couldn't quite break, so she simply accepted it, and smoked less. Life was much easier when you weren't beating up on yourself. Ruscan had taught her that. And how to laugh. But he was gone.

It was dark in the cove, no streetlights to illuminate the dangerous curves and dips of the road. Scattered granite boulders strewn to the sides of the road glowed dimly in the moonlight, while lights flicked on in the houses strung throughout the cove, serving to further emphasize the long stretches of emptiness.

As she settled back into the cool plastic chair, she found herself thinking wistfully that this was the time of day when it was natural to be sitting in quiet companionship with a partner, contemplating the lights of the ferry's last run across the Tickle as it carried the night shift workers into town. A large dark shadow made its meandering way down the rutted lane towards the point—the dog again—out for a solitary evening stroll. Closer at hand, there were a couple of bodies about, heading in the direction of the tiny old church down the road. It was her next-door neighbour, beyond the grove of twisty old lilacs and dogberry trees. She remembered reading the weathered sign outside the building, which proclaimed it to be the Church of St. Jude Without, so it had to be Catholic. The nuns of her childhood would surely approve of her new neighbourhood. She sat up straighter, listening, for the strains of music she could hear were actually coming from the old white and red wooden building, the sound growing and fading each time the main door was opened.

"Is it Wednesday night mass?" she asked aloud as she peered through the leaves. The congregation, what she could see of them, were certainly not dressed in their church best. She could spot the shine of a leather jacket, even through the trees.

As if in answer to her question, a knocking noise sounded—almost a chuckle—from the lilac bush down by the old stump. A large bird rushed out, beating its wings into the night sky, leaving a single branch nodding like the feather in an old-fashioned hat. If she squinted her eyes just so, she could almost see the outline of a man. Like a pirate, maybe.

"Enough already," she muttered, blaming Bridget for planting foolish ideas in her mind. She withdrew back into the old house, carefully avoiding the shadows and closing the door against the smell of boiled cabbage which was drifting on the breeze.

Chapter 2

The early morning air was cool, the sky high and blue. The sun had broken over the easterly mountain, yet dew still shimmered on the unmown grass of the yard. The remnants of what had been a beloved garden ringed the lawn. Hollyhocks, roses, foxgloves and others—their flowers all faded now and dying in the late summer—crowded themselves in a jumble by the house, with only the daisies shining through in the spaces between. Further off, she spotted lines of overgrown greenery in a dug-out patch—a vegetable patch untended yet still producing the root crops leftover from last year. Bushes on the back were spotted with red, green and black berries dripping with ripeness, inviting her to pick them. The dew was deliciously cool on her bare legs and feet as she meandered over, intent on foraging.

The sun warmed her face as she savoured this breakfast, the sweet berries bursting against the sharp tang of yogurt in her mouth. The smell of coffee dripping in the kitchen wafted out and mixed with the heady scent of the late summer woods, warm green notes with a portent of the rot of fall. Was there any more perfect spot on earth to be a hermit?

"You're ready, then," a voice cut through her reverie. Carmel gave herself a quick once-over to double check that she was decently clad—yes, tee shirt and pyjama shorts, then turned to the side yard.

"Bridget," she said, surprised to see her at this early hour. "I didn't take you for a morning person, somehow."

Her neighbour was dressed much as she'd been the day before, but today's Indian cotton dress was dyed in shades of bright yellow grading to orange. The silk embroidery on the fabric shone warmly in the sun with tiny mirrors glinting from among the folds of fabric. Her long hennaed hair was pinned up very loosely with what looked like chopsticks, showing off the fine line of her cheek and neck. Her feet were shod in heavy black boots that had seen much better days.

"It's going to be another hot one," Bridget said. "Until we get a storm to break this weather. There's no shade up on the hill, so I like to get at the berries early." She stood her ground expectantly, and jerked her head towards the mountain high above them.

"Oh, right." Carmel nodded hesitantly, looking up at the high hill stretching far above them. "Yes. Berry picking."

She looked longingly back at her kitchen where the coffee maker was giving its last gurgling cough and the aroma was calling.

"I just need to get changed," she said, indicating her pyjamas. "Why don't you have a coffee while you're waiting?" Carmel looked hopefully at the younger woman, still standing with buckets in her hand. *Good grief,* she thought, *were those salt-beef buckets?* This woman meant business, but Carmel wasn't going anywhere before her morning charge up.

"Sounds good," said Bridget, decisively placing the buckets down on the ground with a grin on her lightly tanned face. She marched up the steps, forcing Carmel to scurry in ahead. Bridget shooed her away with instructions to get ready for the climb, as she expertly manoeuvered herself around Carmel's kitchen, knowing exactly where the mugs and spoons resided. In fact, the younger woman made herself so at home in the kitchen that by the time Carmel returned, steaming cheese omelets awaited them on the table.

She stared at the offering. The aroma wafted around the kitchen and the golden omelets looked perfect. "I just ate…" she said, as she lowered herself to the table reluctantly, really just wanting her coffee. She managed to stuff a few bites in her mouth, for the omelets tasted as delicious as they looked, but she was now full to bursting.

"You have to eat protein too," Bridget said as she dug into her own plate. After that was cleared, she exchanged plates with Carmel and ate the remainder of her portion too.

Later, setting off up the clear trail leading from Carmel's back yard up into the woods, Bridget explained they'd be climbing to the very top of the hill, right to the barrens of rock and scrub. "The berries don't grow in the shade of the trees, you see," she said.

They climbed and climbed, then climbed some more. Through the trees, then a jungle of waist-high bushes, then finally from one rocky ledge to another. From the house, it had looked like an easy path meandering around the rocks and grasses, but Carmel found that the reality was far harsher.

"Isn't there an easier way?" she finally huffed, pausing to lean against a lichen-covered rock face. She lay down the white buckets Bridget had made her carry. "Maybe stairs, or a road perhaps?"

"All wilderness here on in," Bridget said, not even one drop of sweat beading her forehead in the heat of the now strong sun. "We could have gone in the back way, but that would have meant a two-mile hike in our rubber boots. Even in late August, the bogs are something fierce up there."

Carmel squinted up her face at the rocks ahead. "Bogs up this high? Surely they'd drain, what with gravity and... and water finding its own level, and stuff."

"This is pure rock," Bridget said, thumping the closest one. "Probably older than most of North America. She turned back to the barely marked path. "Did you know that this part of the island used to be in Africa?"

Carmel had no breath to reply as she forced herself up and up the rock face, trying to keep pace with the younger woman.

"Okay," said Bridget stopping abruptly. "This is good."

Carmel looked past her new friend to where the mountain had leveled out, relatively speaking, and she could see boulder-strewn grass, with dips and hillocks, for a long way ahead. Even here in late August, there was refreshing greenery of bushes, trees and moss. Above them was only sky. Bridget had talked of a storm heading their way, but the cloudless blue stretched on endlessly.

Bridget led her to a blueberry patch, the low bushes gleaming with bright blue, fat berries. Now that Carmel knew what she was looking for, she couldn't miss the shrubs with their fruit, to be seen all around, in every little hollow.

Every so often, she had to stand up to stretch her back which had become stiff from bending and squatting down to the bushes, and to keep an eye out for her friend, making sure they didn't wander too far from each other. Though there could be little possibility of getting lost, for all she'd need to do is head for the ocean side and climb down the hill, she didn't want to take a chance. After only an hour or so, all four buckets were filled. The sun now beat down on them and

Carmel felt drowsily satisfied at having had such a productive day already.

Bridget led the way back down the mountain, pausing at a rocky ledge just above the treeline. "Let's take a seat for a moment," she said. The two faced the ocean as Bridget broke out the thermos and poured more coffee, the breeze coming up the mountain from the water below, cooling their sun-warmed cheeks. Carmel could see far off to the west at the horizon, the other side of the large bay, and closer—Bell Island looming out with its sheer cliffs, and the other littler island on its southern side. To the north, the land stretched on, so-called barren scrub land of rock and bush, but past that was only ocean right up to Greenland.

She took the plastic cup handed to her, and thought this would be a lovely moment for a cigarette. The warm sun on her back, the aroma of the still fresh coffee, the satisfaction of knowing she'd had more of a workout this morning already than she'd had all last year. If, of course, one still smoked in public, which she didn't do. Fortunately, she hadn't brought her pack with her. She doubted that Bridget, the fit healthy Bridget who'd leaped up the mountainside with no more effort than if it was a flat grassy meadow, would look kindly on her filthy habit. She sighed and leaned back against the rock face, breathing deeply of the mountain-warmed sea air as compensation.

A familiar sound shook her out of her reverie. It was the click and whoosh of a... lighter. An old-fashioned Zippo, if she wasn't mistaken. And there.... Yes, there was the smell of the butane, or diesel, or whatever powered those things.

She started up, eyes open, suddenly wide awake and stared over at Bridget. Leaning back against the warm rock, her neighbour lazily lifted a single brow and offered the cigarette pack her way as she let a steady stream of smoke out of her lungs.

Carmel hesitated, then accepted one. "It's so peaceful up here," Carmel said, leaning back. Her belly full still, with coffee and cigarette in hand with the sun-warmed rock behind her back, it was heaven. She couldn't see her own house from here, hidden behind an outcrop of trees and rock, but the point and the houses on it were visible, and a tiny cottage off down in the woods. The ferry endlessly chugged across the Tickle. "If it weren't for the houses and the ferry, you'd think you were in the wilderness. No sound, not even a scrap of litter."

Bridget murmured her agreement, eyes shut and relaxed against the sun.

"Well, except for the bits of orange tape on the trees down there," Carmel added. "But I wouldn't count them as litter. They're just marking out property."

The effect of her words on Bridget was like an electric start.

"Tape?" Bridget was sputtering. "What tape? What property?" She sat up, glaring down at the trees Carmel was pointing towards.

"This is Crown land here, no one's got any business marking it." Bridget was already on her feet and was striding past the bushes and rocks to inspect the neon markings closer.

When Carmel caught up to her, Bridget was systematically tearing the bits of fluorescent orange plastic from each tree and stuffing them into the pockets of her dress.

"Oh, no, you don't," Bridget was muttering under her breath as she reached another tree. "Not on my watch, you don't. They'd never allow it, you know."

Carmel hesitated. "The government?" she asked. "No, certainly not if it's Crown land, you're not allowed to build on it." She was pretty sure that was correct.

Bridget caught herself in mid-breath, and turned to face Carmel.

"I wish you were right on that," she said in a low voice. "But sometimes the government thinks Crown land is theirs to do with as they wish, not to preserve for the people. They think this whole island is theirs for the taking to get rich from, and don't respect what they should, even those who should know better. Let's go back now," she said, frowning as she abruptly picked up her buckets and turned to the path. She set off down the mountain side stepping firmly in her heavy black boots.

Carmel followed her back to her house, struggling to keep up with the younger woman on the rough paths. She watched as Bridget barely paused to deposit her share of the morning's berries inside her gate then strode off down the road towards the point, her shoulders grimly set.

She turned to look back up the mountain side, wondering why the land above had been marked off by surveyors with their reflective tape. It was a steep incline, the area between her house and the emergence of the granite headland, surely not the greatest for development. And who was Bridget's 'they' who wouldn't allow it to happen? If she'd been talking about residents of the Cove being moved to action against the government, she would surely have said 'we,' being as she was an integral part of the close-knit family in the community. It was a mystery, and Carmel was pretty sure she didn't want any more mysteries in her life. The mystery of Ruscan was enough to last her for a while.

Supper would be light, for the weather was far too warm to think of cooking after the heat of the day, and she still wasn't hungry after the large breakfast Bridget had provided. The air was close and heavy, sucking all energy out of her, and the only things she could conjure from her fridge were the ingredients for a toasted tomato and cheese sandwich. She turned on the television evening news for company, something she'd started to do religiously after Ruscan's disappearance, originally borne of a desperate need to scour every source no matter how slim the chance, of somewhere, somehow, finding clues to his whereabouts, but which had now become a habit.

This rare heat wave was getting to everyone. The news was filled with reports of last night's rioting on George Street, the infamous road of bars in the downtown of the nearby city. Three weeks of thirty degrees and endless sunshine might sound paradisiacal to dwellers of almost anywhere else in the civilized world, but as they were used to the year-round freezing effects of the icy Labrador current, the denizens of St. John's were starting to fray around the edges. Perhaps they were merely going through rain withdrawal, but everyone was fed up with the hot weather. As the TV reporter repeatedly stated, "It's not the heat, it's the humidity."

To make matters worse, in addition to the unseasonable heat, there was a beer strike currently being waged. All the local brewery workers had banded together to demand their dues—higher wages and more vacation time, especially since with global warning the summers were turning hotter. They couldn't have planned a more perfect window of time to withhold their services in quenching the thirst of the land. It had gone on so long that the stores of local beer had dissipated, and the government's own laws meant that none was allowed to be exported in from the other non-striking breweries in the mainland of Canada. The liquor stores carried imported beer, from America and Europe, but these beverages were unpalatable to the average islander, being different in taste and presented in foreign-looking bottles. And so the patrons of George Street, that historical lane made up of forty or more bars, lounges and taverns—these good citizens—were forced to drink rum and were unhappy with that. Unfortunately, they tended to guzzle the liquor down at the same rate they would beer, with the result of very drunken, very unhappy hordes rampaging the downtown streets at night.

The riots had started simply enough, with just a slight increase in calls for the Royal Newfoundland Constabulary, as evidenced in their daily reports sent out to the media. The rising violence was put down to the unseasonably hot and sunny weather which had stretched out through August, normally a month of fog and rain. As the beer supplies sank, however, and the regular patrons began to feel the pinch and the rum, the violence escalated to a point not seen since 1932, when the unemployed, starving mobs brought down the government. The present-day mobs were not protesting political ideals, though, they were just having the most drunken times of their lives.

Glass was scattered everywhere around the downtown. Bottles smashed, shop windows broken, even the iron fence erected to safe-guard visiting ships was torn down manually at the peak of the riots by the hundreds of yobs who swarmed the downtown streets. The general mob reasoning for this last act was that the fence prevented them from their God-given right of enjoying strolls along their own waterfront, and they may have had a point. No less than seven bodies were pulled out of the harbour that night, all of them still breathing, yet not noticeably sobered up by their dunk in the dirty harbour waters.

Reporters were flown in from all points of the continent and beyond to witness the nightly devastations, and professors from the university gave their learned opinions as to the root cause of the rioting. Meanwhile, the provincial government, which understood the true situation, scurried to get the unions and brewery management talking. It was their misfortune that neither side really wanted to parlay yet, though, for all were enjoying the unexpectedly lengthened summer break from work. Carmel laughed as she switched off the television.

She brought her evening cup of tea outside, in order to enjoy the sunset. It could become a comfortable habit, this taking tea after supper on the veranda. She glanced about her at the cove and its houses scattered along the road in the gathering dusk. Much as usual, although one thing stuck out, literally. A large black SUV had been parked down the road to her right. Well, not so much parked as left in the middle of the road, as if the owner didn't care to share. Another vehicle would just barely be able to squeeze by. The emergency lights weren't flashing, and it wasn't near any house. She briefly wondered who would be so rude as to leave their car like that.

Bridget appeared on her doorstep again, her mood much brighter than when she'd left that morning. She carried an empty beer tankard in each hand.

"Come on over to the church," Bridget invited her. "The crowd's all there."

Carmel thought back on the music and people of the previous night.

"Sure," she said. "Is there a Bingo game on?"

Bingo was the only activity she could think of that might be held in the church in the evening, these places usually being reserved for worship services.

"Bingo?" Bridget laughed as if Carmel had made a joke. "This crowd doesn't play bingo." She saw the confusion on Carmel's face. "No, no, you've got it wrong." She surprised her by hooking her arm into Carmel's who tried not to flinch at the unexpected touch. Her dress was made of soft red velvet tonight, still in the loose hippy style. It was impossible to tell what Bridget's figure was like, the way she dressed. Still, she hadn't gotten out of breath on their morning's climb up the mountain, so Carmel had to assume she was pretty fit.

"Sid's father bought the church thirty years back when they deconsecrated it," Bridget told her as they made their way to the road and next door. "He used it for storage, but when he passed on, Sid realized his lifelong dream and made it into a bar. He quit his job with the Coast Guard and came on home."

"But there's no sign up," Carmel objected. "At least, not a sign saying it's a bar—only the old church sign. No neon, not even lights outside. How are people supposed to know it's a place of business?"

Bridget squinted at her with an uncomprehending look infused with an element of pitying.

Carmel sighed in exasperation at her new friend. "How does he make money, or attract people here?" she asked, having to spell it out. "How does he encourage business?"

"Well, he doesn't need to, does he?" Bridget said. "We all know he's here, and when the stained glass window is lit up, that means he's open." She pointed above their heads. There, under the steeple was a rose window, the reds and blues glowing dimly in a petal pattern. It was much smaller than any Carmel had seen in the cathedrals in Europe, of course—more of a rosette really—but sweet in its simplicity.

The church itself was a testament to a simpler time. The west facing rosette was the only extravagance, paid for by parishioners years ago to honour some long forgotten happening. The clapboard was once painted white and now flaked from the salt sea air, its bell tower overlooking the Cove from the promontory. The top of the steeple came to a point with a rusted wind vane, unmoving in the sultry late summer air. Three arched windows graced the side of the church, and Carmel could see these were plain glass, old glass, the ripples in the glass evident even from where she stood. A single small extension was visible at the very back—the east side.

Bridget held the front door open, and gestured Carmel to follow her through the porch created by the bell tower and into the body of the former church. Although a small space, the raised pitch of the ceiling helped the single room feel more spacious than it truly was. Looking up, Carmel could see the thick rafters and the planks which made up the roof itself, once painted the pea green so beloved of the Victorians, now faded in the dull gloom. The walls below had been white washed, but not within recent memory.

Two lights over a pool table to their right showed a group of men desultorily hitting balls across the worn green felt with wooden cues, more interested in their loud banter than keeping score. An old fashioned pinball machine lay in waiting, its lights flashing enticingly, but no sound came from it. Noticeably absent also were the ever-pervasive video gambling machines. In fact, the only sounds were the muted ancient rock music and the comfortable murmur of old friends at leisure, with the exception of the pool players who were becoming raucous with drink. Nobody seemed to mind.

A group of bikers sat in the corner minding their own business. They were all dressed identically in black leather jackets and baseball caps. On the back of the closest jacket she could pick out an embroidered motif of a white skull wearing a wide-brimmed hat with a feather. Rather a whimsical choice for tough guys.

Off to the left, some people were sitting amongst the mishmash of pews, tables and chairs, while an ancient iron wood stove idled, its top used now as a repository for empty glasses and discarded chip bags but looking capable of heating the entire room when the long winter set in. The much scuffed wooden floor planks, also once painted white long ago, were at least eight inches wide, an indication of the building's age. Straight ahead to the eastern aspect of the old church, Carmel saw a large arched opening which led to the addition she'd seen from the outside. This small space, totally open on the side of the main body of the church, was not big enough to be called a separate room but was long enough to hold another arched window each side, with a smaller window at the very back. This was where the altar would have been, and now appeared to be used as the bar. She surmised this not because of the presence of bottles because there were none visible, but rather because of the lights. White Christmas lights and other multi-coloured LEDs framed the tiny sanctuary, and even the bar itself glowed, under lighting the faces of the few men standing around it. Carmel ran her hand along it—it seemed to be made of a stone so thin the light below the bar shone through.

"Sid," Bridget nodded to the man behind the bar as she claimed the only available two bar stools. Carmel's stool wobbled when she touched it, so she sat very gingerly. She wouldn't want to be too drunk while sitting on this—it was swaying beneath her even in a sober state.

"This is Carmel. She's living in Uncle Frank's house next door," Bridget said by way of introducing Carmel to the community. The men closest to them nodded in Carmel's direction then went back to their drinks and talk. This lack of reaction to a stranger in their midst surprised her. It was not that she found them rude, or that she was under any illusions that people would be fascinated by her, but in her travels around the globe she'd learned that people in very small places tended to latch on to new faces mostly out of curiosity, enticed by the fresh blood. Carmel mentioned this to her companion, whose brow furrowed as she tried to explain.

"You're a woman, and they don't know you yet, so it would be bad manners," she said. "Besides, you might only be here for a short time, so it doesn't make sense for them to invest the energy to get to know you. You're not part of the Cove yet."

This answer discomfited her, she didn't quite know why, but she held on to the 'yet' as a positive sign of future acceptance.

Sid the barkeep stood in front of them. He towered over them, lean and long, holding a commanding presence over the whole bar, his shrewd eyes keeping watch like a priest with his flock. He also had the most magnificent moustache Carmel had ever seen, like the walrus in Alice in Wonderland, the sides drooping out from his face and up in the air again. His hand absentmindedly stroked it as he asked them if it was beer they were wanting that evening. Without waiting for a reply, he opened two beer bottles, took the tankards from where Bridget had laid them and poured the beers. He placed them back in front of the women along with a fresh bowl of peanuts, and then turned back to the group of men on his right.

Bridget laid a five dollar bill on the counter, but put her hand out to stop Carmel when she did the same.

"No," she said. "Five is plenty. Beer's cheap here. You can get the next round."

Carmel looked around at the old hall. Everyone was drinking out of mugs, glasses and tankards, like themselves, with nary a beer bottle in sight. The beer strike devastating the rest of the province didn't seem to have affected this small bar. In fact, that's all anyone was drinking as there weren't any liquor bottles on display behind the bar. Had the bar keep stockpiled a stash of ale before the brewery strike? She peered at a bottle left on the counter. The writing seemed to be in French, which meant it came in from another province (or country, for the tiny island of St. Pierre was much closer than Quebec, geographically speaking). She leaned in for a closer look, but it was quickly whisked out of her sight. Carmel looked up to meet Sid's baleful glare.

Two men entered through a side door, bringing with them the sweet smell of cigarettes. When the building was a church, that door would have led to a graveyard, surely. "There's a graveyard out there, isn't there?" she asked Bridget. Her house was next door, not leaving a lot of room between the two structures for a burial ground.

"It's up around behind your house," Bridget told her through a mouthful of peanuts. "The church is all built on rock, the closest bit of topsoil is up in the woods."

"Okay," Carmel nodded. "That makes sense—that must have been where the kids were playing with a flashlight last night. Just the sort of thing that teenagers would love."

"What kids are those?"

Carmel turned towards the new voice, and her tankard froze halfway to her mouth. Here was possibly the most gorgeous man she'd ever seen off a movie screen, coming towards them from the direction of the pool table. Standing between the two women, all six foot two of him, his broad shoulders blocked any view of the room behind him. Carmel got the impression of blond shaggy curls, slightly graying at the temples, with the weathered lines on his chiselled face showing he must be in his mid-forties. Even in the dim light, she could see his eyes were a startling blue. And his lips... Oh, it was a purely visceral reaction she was feeling. Like a punch, she could sense the warmth from his body and could feel her own response, an inevitable melting. She breathed in deep the better to gather the smell of beer and cigarettes and that slight almost animal musk, the smell of a working man who sweats honestly and wears it like a badge. She'd never felt this before, the sudden intoxication of a powerful physical attraction. Not even with Ruscan, her best friend with whom she'd developed love (and he was gone).

"There you are," Bridget lightly scolded the newcomer. "I went down to your place looking for you today." She hugged him close and kissed him on his bristly cheek.

"Out on the boat," he said, hugging her back. The low rumbling of his deep voice at such close quarters was awakening something deep inside Carmel. She flushed and tried to ignore it, holding on to the cool glass tankard with both hands. Perhaps this was early menopause, *this warmth must be the hot flashes women talked about,* she thought feverishly. And this must be the fisherman she'd seen coming into the wharf. How could Bridget stand so close to him, how could she treat him so casually without fainting?

"Phonse, this is Carmel." Bridget let go of him. Suddenly a few things appeared much clearer. Out of a habit born from organizing her thoughts for writing, she began a mental list. One, this was Roxanne's landlord. No wonder the English woman had been all atwitter. This seething mass of physical masculinity was enough to change the bluest stocking into a flapper. Two, obviously this was Bridget's man, hence why the younger woman had looked rather put out, she thought, remembering back to the evening before. And three, remembering how Bridget had raged at whoever had placed orange markers on the trees that afternoon, Carmel stopped counting and shivered. No way was she going to step on this woman's toes about a man, even this man. She might look like a peaceful hippy-chick, but underneath that flowing hennaed hair lurked a purely feline territoriality.

Phonse's eyes lit on Carmel and he smiled. It cut through her like glass, exposing every nerve, she had to look away. Yes, if Bridget with her airiness was his partner, then Roxanne wouldn't be his type at all. She swallowed and held up her hand in greeting so he wouldn't try to shake it, not trusting herself not to melt if he touched her.

"Hey," she grunted in a studiedly casual manner. Her cheeks further inflamed.

His eyebrow cocked up a notch as his grin grew. *Shoot!* she thought. *Can he read my mind?*

"You mentioned kids—have they been bothering you?" he asked, then took a swallow from his glass.

"Oh, no!" she said, giving herself a mental shake. Using a line she'd once heard on the radio, she told herself firmly that the least she could do was pretend to be normal. "No, no bother. I just mentioned that they must have been playing in the graveyard last night."

She thought she saw Bridget and Phonse share a quick glance. He reached past the two women to grab a handful of nuts.

"Doubt that," Phonse said as he chewed thoughtfully. "All the youngsters old enough to be out at that hour in the Cove were gone to town last night to the movies. What did you see out there?"

"Just some lights through the trees," Carmel replied. "The kids were laughing and playing, it was no bother."

Carmel looked up from her beer to see Bridget mouthing something at Phonse. They both looked at her sharply, then too casually glanced away.

"What is it?" Carmel asked.

Phonse drew a breath to reply when Bridget quickly cut in.

"I wanted to tell you today," she said, looking at Phonse. "We found some orange marking tape tied to trees up in the woods."

Whatever he'd planned to say was ripped away by this news.

"The bastards!" A storm gathered in his intense eyes, the handsome brow lowered. "So it's true, eh?"

Bridget nodded somberly. "Looks like it," she replied. She glanced at Carmel and explained, "We've been hearing rumours of a development planned for those woods up there, and up the mountain."

Phonse made as if to spit. "Mansions on the cliff face," he said in disgust. "As if that could ever fly."

"You know they can do it," she said quietly.

"Taking Crown land for their own profit," Phonse added. He swigged the last from his heavy glass tankard.

"But Crown land is untouchable, surely," Carmel said. "No one is allowed to build on it."

"Not if the government sells it to them," Bridget replied in a bitter tone. "And in this case, the developer is the premier's brother. The government makes the law, and they can change it to suit their own whims."

Carmel thought of the lovely wooded area behind her house, sad to think of it torn down for oversized mansions of the rich. She sighed. There was no stopping the push for expansion.

The cove residents weren't going to take the passive line, however.

"That does it," said Phonse. "Time to take action."

He thumped the glass on the bar, calling for attention from all. Sid flicked a button and the ever present Credence Clearwater Revival muted.

"Listen up," he ordered. He glanced around the room to ensure he had everyone's attention. "They've started that nonsense about the development again."

Groans and curses were heard throughout the small hall. One man stood up from the table he'd been occupying alone, in the back. A large black dog sat at attention by his side, glaring around the room.

"Over my dead body!" he roared. "If that god damn townie shows his face in this cove it'll be the last thing he does!"

Rumblings of agreement echoed throughout, and several voices shouted out what they, too would do if given the opportunity.

"Well, Clyde," replied Phonse, hands on his hips. "I don't think we need to resort to violence, but we have to do something to protect it."

"Building them big monster mansions all on top of each other, there'll be no shoreline left soon enough," the man called Clyde continued. "Not to mention the harm it'll do my farm. They'll screw up the water table and the runoff will kill us all."

This must be the owner of the farm north of the small community, the hopeful source of Carmel's future local groceries. He looked as if he hadn't shaved for a while—or washed either—with his wild hair sticking off at every angle from his balding pate.

"That there farm," he continued, spit flying, finger pointing in the farm's direction. "That farm has been there more'n two hundred years. It were *my* family chased the French away from here, and the Beothuk, and claimed it for us. It's my land, and they'll not be messing with it, nor me!"

"Okay, Clyde, we know," Phonse attempted to shut the man up so they could start discussing their options.

"I'll club the bastard across his fat head," Clyde muttered, sitting back down on his pew. A fit of coughing overtook him, preventing him from embellishing that thought.

Just then, the front entrance opened with a whoosh and a large man swept inside. Six foot tall and almost that around, his well-fed body was dressed all in white, not the garb of a man who works for a living. Heavy gold flashed at his wrist, neck and fingers. Even from this distance and dim light, his cheeks shone as though polished. He paused at the doorway, ensuring he was seen, before shutting the door.

"The weather is waiting, boys," he said, starting up towards the bar, rubbing his hands together as if in glee. "Waiting for a storm."

He nodded greetings to those he passed. They were not returned. Where moments before, the hall was in an uproar, it was now pitch quiet, and every face turned to stone.

"Well, hello, little ladies," the man said as he ran an appreciative eye over the two women at the bar. "A drink for me and my friends, Sid, my boy!" The strong smell of his sickly aftershave washed over them, making Carmel want to vomit.

The music blared suddenly, warning all about the bad moon a-rising. Sid slowly turned around to face the newcomer. The glowing bar lit up his face, throwing his hooded eyes in shadow. He wordlessly poured a bottle into a flimsy plastic cup, placed it on the counter, and held out his hand for payment.

"Start a tab for me there, Sid," the man said. When the bartender silently remained in position with his hand out, the man rolled his eyes and fished a ten dollar bill out of his wallet, tossing it lightly on the bar. Sid took the money and rang into the hitherto unused cash register that Carmel hadn't even noticed. A few coins in change were dropped on the bar next to the large man, which he pointedly ignored.

Sid busied himself pouring another into Phonse's large glass. As the gorgeous man took a swallow, Carmel could see the heat in Phonse's reddened face, the fire smoldering in his eyes. He didn't look very sober. How much had he already drunk? She'd been too entranced by his physical presence to notice earlier.

"You're not welcome here, Peters," he said in a low voice, slurred with emotion.

"Alphonse, Alphonse, it's a public place," said the newcomer with false bonhomie dripping from his very words. "Besides, I'll soon be your neighbour again." His berry eyes narrowed in spite as he sneered at Phonse. The man's white hair glowed greenish in the LED Christmas lights.

"Yup," he said, pointing to the back of the old church, to the woods and the graveyard beyond. "That's all gonna be mine, you know. And I'm gonna move all my friends up there. And this sweet little cove is gonna be the best goddamn marina closest to town."

He thumped his cup on the bar for emphasis, without the intended effect however, for the liquid merely sloshed quietly out of the plastic, spilling onto the stone bar.

"Don't worry, Phonse, my old trout," Peters continued. "There'll be work for you. You can give up the fishing. I'll let you swab down my yacht!"

The fat bastard chortled to himself, and he didn't even see Phonse's arm flash up to meet his nose. He staggered and rolled, but like a roly-poly punching bag, he didn't fall.

"I'll have you up for that, you freakin' good-for-nothing- fisherman!" Peters screamed, all false jolliness now dropped as the blood streamed from his nose. He attempted to stem the flow but it dripped down the front of his linen suit. He whipped a snowy white hanky out of his breast pocket, as he stomped heavily down the hall and out of the old church building.

Phonse flexed his fist, grimacing as he did so.

"You shouldn't have done that, Phonse," Carmel heard Bridget whisper furiously.

Sid snorted. "Someone had to," he said. "That arse is lucky he didn't get worse."

Chapter 3

Carmel checked the pie's progress through the dirty oven window. The whole stove could do with a good cleaning, but that was a job to put off till winter. Right now she was only concerned with her pie and its lovely, lustrous golden pastry. The hot aroma engulfed her as she pulled the oven door down.

"Oh yeah," she murmured as she breathed in deeply and lifted it clear of the oven. Unfortunately, the smell of the pie didn't match its appearance, with purple juice bubbling out of the vents and along the imperfectly sealed bit where the top met the base. Although Carmel loved to cook and prided herself on her skill in the kitchen, even she had to admit that she rarely had the patience to perfectly follow a recipe. She invariably found herself taking short cuts which usually failed, or forgetting to add a vital ingredient. Like tapioca or corn starch—in fact, anything to thicken the pie filling. Puddles of juice lay dripping and boiling along the oven floor.

Still, it was the taste that was important, and the smell, and the crunch of the buttery pastry baked to perfection. She set it on the wire rack laid out by the open window and gazed proudly upon her creation. Today, the planets were all aligned for she had met a gorgeous man last night (yes, he was Bridget's, but a girl could fantasize, couldn't she?) and the pastry itself was well-made. Life flowed through her veins.

The smell must have attracted the cat back, though there was no way he was going to get any pie. His white-streaked nose pushed at the window screen, and his claws made a rasping noise against it as if he was determined to rip his way through the offensive barrier.

"No," she cried, and ran through the back door to chase him off.

He jumped lightly down, paused to make eye contact to show he took no offense, then began to saunter leisurely away. After ten feet, he stopped, looked back at her and chirruped, almost as if he was inviting her to join him.

It has been said that the lives of cats are curious things. While they sleep a full two-thirds of their lives away, the remainder is spent in secret meanderings of thought and action which might make no sense to the average human. Carmel wondered where he lived. This was no stray cat, for he was definitely well-fed and looked as if he was regularly and lovingly groomed by a brush. He chirruped again, louder this time.

"Okay," she said to him, making up her mind as she shoved her feet into her sneakers without lacing them up. "I'm free; you lead. I'm right behind you. Show me the neighbourhood."

Glad there was no one there to witness the foolishness of her walking with a cat, she trotted off after him for she was curious as to where he spent his days. He glanced behind him occasionally as if to make sure she hadn't gotten lost. Being a cat, he would lose interest soon enough and dart off under bushes where she couldn't follow, but Carmel was happy enough to play his game as long as it lasted. Through the bushes, then the trees, till they came to a small glade.

The leaves of the tall trees filtered the sunlight, dappling the grass as if in a woodland cathedral, and the warm air hummed with bees. Ancient gravestones of white granite, their writing eaten by years of salt wind, leaned into the grassy hummocks as though they'd always been there. The grass looked like it had been mown within the past month—of course, the descendants of the grave yard still lived in St. Jude Without, and would, no doubt, keep up the old ways of honouring their forebears. Within the grassy meadow, a perfect circle was etched out, and Carmel didn't need to look closer to realize it was a fairy-ring, created by the sprouting of mushrooms from a single spore. She spotted the cat sitting atop a small base of stone, the pillar lying next to it, long ago toppled.

Then a voice of inhuman loveliness filled the warm space, its notes drifting effortlessly through the haunting tune of an Irish ballad, a song of love and loss and pain. She recognized the tune, but not the words, for they weren't English nor any language she could recognize. Perhaps the original Celtic? She shivered deep within, despite the warmth of the day. Then drowsiness overcame her. The air was still and thick.

Carmel felt the need to sit for a spell, and sank down into the welcoming grass, the better to listen, the sound lulling her, wrapping her into a memory of hot summer days long ago, touching a chord of longing within. It wasn't a human voice, it was the sound of the land, of the ancients and their spirits of ancient times. She could weep with the mourning of pain within it, or... just lay her head down on the soft sun warmed granite...

A rustle caused her to sit up with a start. How long had she been lying there? She lifted her head to see the large tuxedo cat gracefully leap into the arms of a very ordinary woman, a very old woman. Two dark eyes gazed at Carmel from deep within her leathered face. *She could be a witch from a storybook*, Carmel thought, *except for her clothes.* The woman wore a very ordinary, cheap-looking nylon top with red poppies emblazoned on it, and a pair of men's cotton workpants, well-worn but fairly clean.

"I didn't know you was there, m'dear," the woman said with such a strong smooth voice it didn't seem possible to come from the withered crone. "You awake now?"

She peered down from a great height at Carmel, who scrambled to her feet.

"Did you hear the singing?" Carmel whispered, still trying to shake off the feeling the music had cast on her, almost like an enchantment.

"Sorry about that," the old one answered, huffily now, pulling herself up to her full height. "Like I said, I didn't know you was there. It's not my fault if folks goes tramping where they're not supposed to."

Carmel stared at her, confused. "It was you?" She stared about her. "I didn't know this was private property. I thought it was the graveyard. I was just following the cat..."

The flint-black eyes softened at once. The woman's face was all of a sudden not so scary.

"It were Hank brought you here, was it?" the old woman asked. "That's all right then. He told me about you."

The old woman must be a little deaf, she decided. Carmel wasn't sure if she'd met a Hank in the bar last night. There had been a lot of people—one of them might have been Hank.

"No, the cat..." she began in a louder voice, a little embarrassed to explain that she'd been whimsically following the cat. "I fed him last night, and was just wondering where he lived..."

"Yes, that was a generous piece of fish, indeed," the woman nodded. "Although he do prefer it fresher. He ate it out of politeness to you."

She chuckled and scratched the cat under his chin. He purred in satisfaction, a great rumbling low motor, flashing his devilish grin at Carmel.

Had the old crone been spying on her? That would explain the presence she'd felt in the back yard last night.

"They call me Melba," the woman said.

"Like the opera singer?" Carmel asked. "If that was your voice, then I can see why."

Melba gave another warm chuckle. *Really*, Carmel thought, *I would never place that rich voice with the great age of the woman, and perhaps not so deaf after all.*

"You're a quick one," she said. "I was christened Mary Assumpta, but the priest called me Melba as soon as he heard me sing, and it stuck."

"And the cat?" Carmel asked, still trying to figure out who Hank was.

"Yes, that's Hank," Melba told her. "Just plain old Hank. He loves it when I sing for the fairies, you know."

Ookay. There was a problem. The woman, despite her gorgeous voice, was a little doo-lally, and dementia took a lot of different forms. "Do you live around here?" she asked the old lady gently.

"Just through there," she replied, pointing through the trees, away from the direction of Carmel's new home.

"So you'll be affected by the development too," Carmel said, looking back up at the woods behind them. "Such a shame; this is a beautiful private spot. But that's the price of progress, I guess."

The change in her companion's face was unexpected and total. Where tenderness had sat, now reigned rage and a deep anger. A string of curses followed the sparks flying from her eyes and the intensity in her voice electrified the small grove. With a perturbed expression on his face, the cat jumped from her arms back on to the safety of his granite perch.

"And damn him and his brother to hell!" Melba shouted. "I knew his mother and she'd be turning in her grave if she knew what was afoot! I helped raise those boys when they came to the Cove, but if I'd known then their evil I would have cast them into the fires as the devil's spawn!"

She leaned down closer to Carmel, her voice lowered but no less intense.

"We are the stewards of the land, the good Lord said," Melba continued, her black eyes piercing into Carmel's wide open blue ones. "And those that act against him shall be smote onto the rocks and cliffs leading to Hell itself."

She straightened up to her full height and offered a hand to Carmel who quickly scrambled to stand. Good Lord! Despite her age, the woman towered over her by a good three inches, and her hand grasped Carmel's solidly. *How old was she?* Carmel wondered. Eric Peters looked to be in his late fifties, if not early sixties, and if Melba had been his babysitter, she would be at least, what? Seventy-five? Despite her wrinkled face and possible unstable mental status, physically the woman was strong as an ox.

Melba nodded as she peered down into Carmel's eyes. "And you, you've come to help," the woman said, her voice still thundering through the quiet graveyard. "Stranger you might be, but *they* brought you here, the fey. See that you do your part."

With that, the woman turned and left, hurrying down a path that Carmel could have sworn was not there a moment before, as if it had magically opened up to her intentions, with Hank, the cat, following close at her heels. The air hung heavy and still, all insects silent, yet the peace that had been in the grove was gone for Carmel now.

This encounter left Carmel shaken and out of sorts for the rest of the day. The old woman named Melba was obviously not in her full wits, and she wondered if Bridget or any of the others realized the extent of her dementia. Still, in a small community like this, everyone tended to know each other's business, and no doubt kept an eye on the woman. She appeared to be fairly well-kept, despite her odd garb, and strong enough to show she was eating regularly.

"I wonder where I'll be when I'm her age," Carmel said, looking at her mirror by the back door in her kitchen. Sometimes it scared her, the thought of growing old and probably alone, if her life so far was any indication. "Will there be anyone to keep an eye out for me?"

With no children in her life, and never having cultivated close friendships in her lone travels, the future could look very dark if one dwelled on those sorts of things. And hermits lived a long time, didn't they?

"The point of power is now," Carmel took a deep breath while mentally voicing the mantra she'd used for herself in years past when anxiety threatened. "I can change things from this point forward." She paused while she tried to think just *how* she could change the situation of her life.

"Make more friends," she told herself sternly, forgetting about the vow of solitude she'd recently taken. "Be friendlier, more open and expansive, less judgemental?" She ended on a question mark. And then looked critically at herself in the mirror.

"Get back to the pre-forty weight," she also said to herself, starting to list off things which she wanted to change, forgetting that she was now judging herself harshly when she'd just vowed to stop doing that to others.

"And that means exercise," she said aloud. "Yesterday's hike up the mountain was a good start. Tonight after supper, instead of cake I'll take a walk, perhaps to the farm at the end of the road."

She could kill two birds with one stone, and arrange for fresh milk, eggs and vegetables from Clyde, whose family history on the farm stretched back two hundred years. He had been in a bad mood last night, but would surely soften for a local paying customer.

The dishes done, Carmel set out into the heat of the evening. She paused as she crossed the bridge. A steady stream of water rushed down the chasm of jagged rocks leading to the ocean a short distance away. The solid bedrock was split in two, right up the mountain as if rendered apart by a lightning strike. She wondered what great forces of upheaval caused the fissure, and shivered at the thought of falling from the rickety wooden bridge. It took effort to push through the humid air lying so still and heavy, and Carmel was beginning to sweat as she walked up the incline to the farm's gate. Signs attempted to discourage her from going further by proclaiming the land was private property and no hikers were allowed past the gate. One explicitly told the reader that the land was not, nor ever had been, part of the East Coast Trail.

"He certainly gets his point across," Carmel murmured to herself. "Glad I'm a customer, not a hiker." She pushed past the rusted gate, which screeled as it fell back into place.

Tramping up the laneway, she didn't want to startle him, so she began to call out.

"Clyde?" she queried to the empty farm yard. She could hear the cows in the barn, and the squawking of chickens beyond. It was the picture of bucolic peace, a rare oasis of agriculture on this island of wave-washed stone.

Without warning, a large black furry blur rushed furiously at her, all teeth and deep growls. It happened so suddenly she didn't have time to defend herself, and she found herself flat on her back with a dark furry devil drooling his snarls in her face. She was petrified, unable to move and unwilling to anger the beast further.

"Gerroff 'er!" she heard Clyde's voice cry out what felt like an hour later. "Down, sir!" he roared. The creature backed off a short way, continuing a low threatening growl from the back of his throat.

She slowly sat up, still afraid to make any sudden movement which might loosen the tenuous hold the farmer had over the beast.

"You get out of here! Can ya not read?" Clyde now shouted at her. "It's not land for tramping over."

"It... it... I'm Carmel," she could barely speak. "From Frank Ryan's cottage," she continued in explanation. "Not a hiker," she said, desperate for him to call the dog off to a safer distance. "I want to buy eggs..."

"I don't sell," Clyde scowled. He didn't look like he had changed his clothes from the previous night, and the stubble on his chin still bristled. He hefted the shotgun by his side as if readying himself to use it. "Not worth it to me selling an egg here, an egg there. I sell to the Co-op, and that's enough. Don't want strangers coming up using every excuse to get in here."

The dog gave two short deep barks, echoing his master's words.

"Get out!" Clyde indicated the gate with the gun. "Next time, mind your manners and don't come where you're not wanted."

There was no dignified way to exit the farm, so Carmel didn't even bother trying. She backed away, heart still thumping in her chest, and only began to run when the gate was firmly closed behind her.

So far today she'd met a crazy old woman who
communicated with fairies, and had been threatened
with a gun and a mad dog. Carmel was quickly learning
that St. Jude Without was not the peaceful small cove
she had naively imagined when she'd moved in. She
reached her house, all out of breath from her flight, her
heart still thumping in her chest, and threw herself
down on the steps leading to her veranda. In the vista
which lay before her, the sun was just setting amid a
glorious sky of burning red streaked with pink and
violet, the Tickle below calm as a duck pond, not even
a ferry to break the quiet. It all felt unreal, as if she'd
stumbled from a horror movie into a dreamscape of
unnatural stillness.

"What next?" she asked herself aloud, dazed. Then
her eyes came to rest on the black BMW SUV parked
on the road across from the church. That must belong to
Eric Peters, the man who wanted to develop the
mountain side and woods which made her home so
private. The man who, if you listened to the people in
the bar last night, wanted to rip the community apart,
ruin the watershed and claim the working wharf for a
rich man's playground. He had parked again as if he
owned the whole cove, hardly leaving space on the
narrow road for another vehicle to pass.

She glanced over to the church which was the bar
belonging to the enigmatic Sid. If Peters was in there
again tonight, it was sure to be a sideshow. Hadn't she
had enough negativity thrown her way for one evening?
On the other hand, she was determined to make friends,
if only to stave off loneliness in her old age, and she
could start tonight.

"Oh, admit it," she muttered to herself. "I'm too
nosy not to go over." And besides, there was a chance
that the luscious Phonse would be there. Yes, yes, he

appeared to belong to the ferociously intense and odd Bridget, but still...

Carmel ran inside to change, as her shirt and pants were streaked with dirt and saliva from her encounter with Clyde and his dog. She took a quick glance at her hair, completely fuzzed out from the hot humid weather, and groaned. A quick comb-through with her fingers in an attempt to create the mess into an artistic arrangement didn't work, so she gave up and gathered it back with a scrunchie. Carmel chose the lightest cotton dress in her wardrobe, a white eyelet affair that managed to be sweet yet rather sexy at the same time. Loose in the middle to disguise last winter's bulge still clinging on her hips and belly, but flared and showing off her tanned legs. *Okay,* she thought as she grabbed the largest mug she could find, *I'm ready for the world again.*

The cooler air hit her as soon as she stepped out the front door. A breeze was springing up from the water, and she breathed deeply of the refreshing air. The sun had almost entirely set, the violet clouds now moving quickly through the sky, turning to black above the mountain behind her.

Inside the bar, all was much the same as the previous night, with the exception of the added presence of Peters. He and Roxanne were engrossed in an intense conversation in the darkened corner pew. They were an oddly-matched couple, her so short and him so large and wide. They didn't look up as Carmel entered. After she'd passed the two, she changed her mind and turned back, intent on joining the two for she wanted to hear firsthand what Peters' plans were for the land adjoining her rented property. But too late. Roxanne was already slipping through the door, and Peters was turning to the men at the next table.

Again dressed all in white as if he'd never done a day's work in his life, face scrubbed shiny and cheeks rosy, Peters had already latched onto a new audience, and he was lecturing the men at the next table. Three sheets to the wind and swaying, he seemed to have come back to finish what he'd started the night before. Like an old-time preacher in his pulpit, his voice rose and he shook his finger at the people assembled before him in the body of the church. Even the pool players paused to watch. The seventies band Trooper was advising the patrons to "raise a little hell" through the sound system, and that appeared to be just what Peters was doing.

She spied Bridget at a table full of bikers, sitting on the lap of the one with the flattest belly, his arm around her. Seeing Carmel, she gave the man a quick peck on the cheek and turned to join her. Phonse didn't seem too bothered by Bridget's behaviour, busy as he was holding up the bar and nose-deep in a bag of chips. The white of his t-shirt glowed in contrast to his tanned and muscled arms, and Carmel could feel her heart melt a little inside. As he watched her walk up to them, his eyes drifted over her sweet (yet sexy) dress and a lazy grin spread across his face. When their eyes met, he gave a small wink and nod of his head, so imperceptible a movement she might have imagined it, had all her attention not been focused on the man. She could feel the blush start from her neck, rising excruciatingly through her cheeks and could only hope the dim lights of the bar were hiding the worst of it. *Oh God*, she thought, *is it that obvious I've developed a crush on him?*

"I can't believe he came back here after last night," she said as she approached Bridget and Phonse, nodding her head back at Peters. "Does he live in the cove?"

"He's from here, sort of," Bridget answered, oblivious to the drama playing deep within Carmel. "His mother lived here... there were difficulties in their family, as I understand it. The boys lived at the Orphanage for a while. Their father was a drunk. Lot of violence in the family, and the boys paid the price. But they've done well for themselves since then, one went to law school and is now the premier, the other... well, you've seen him."

The orphanages had been run by religious denominations in the city, Carmel knew, but few of the children in their care had been true orphans. Many had sought temporary refuge there while their families sorted their difficulties out. She knew this because she herself had been dropped off with the nuns at the age of five, almost casually when her mother set off on her travels. Not at an orphanage with other children, but with the Sisters of Mercy in their small convent nestled within the river valley. She'd had a hard time adjusting at first to this change, especially because of Sister Mary Oliphant. A large woman, she'd worn a mantle of anger and had taken a strong dislike to the little girl when she had, in her childish innocence, mispronounced Sister Mary Oliphant's name. Carmel remembered those first few months as a bleak unhappy time, a shadow she skipped over in her memory, a time of cellars and dark places and whispers of the darby-boos, those evil black creatures who ate bad children. But then, Sister Mary Oliphant had miraculously disappeared, and Sister Constantine had taken over her care. With her laughter, her joy and encouragement, Sister Constantine had created good memories in place of the bad. Carmel had hardly even noticed when her mother was reported killed in the Sudan and, except for a crumpled photo, she would have long forgotten what she looked like. Sister Constantine she still kept in touch with.

"Why do you ask?" Bridget asked, bringing her back into the present day.

"I met Melba, my neighbour," Carmel replied. "She's really upset by what Peters is doing."

"Well, she can't let..." Phonse said.

"She has a lot to lose," Bridget firmly spoke over him at the same time. They glanced at each other and looked away.

"Nobody's very happy about this development business, are they?" Carmel questioned. "Is it the fact that they'll be building and ripping out the woods, or is it the man behind it that has upset everyone?"

Bridget looked at her with a strange smile.

"Well, let's say a little of both," she suggested. "We're happy here in the cove, just the way it is."

"We like our privacy," Phonse added, with a gleam in his eye. Another small look passed between the two, then Bridget took Carmel's mug and turned to Sid to order another round.

Phonse took this opportunity to lean forward and loosely place an arm around Carmel's shoulder. Her world swayed just a little—she couldn't tell if it was Phonse's effect on her, the amount he'd drunk or her rickety stool. She could definitely smell the beer on his breath. "Why don't you come down to the boat sometime and I'll take you out on the water?" he asked, the warmth of his breath tickling her neck. "Maybe a day trip to Bell Island?"

Her heart jumped into her mouth, leaving no room for words with which to answer. Was he asking her out while Bridget had momentarily turned her back? Perhaps, it was just wishful thinking on her part, and she gave herself a mental shake. Not only was he a fine physical specimen, he was a kind, thoughtful man, offering to take a newcomer around to show her the sights. She darted a glance at her friend, who by this time stood watching the pair, one eyebrow lifted. Bridget gave a sharp flick with her head as if ordering him away.

Phonse cleared his throat, arm dropping to his side and mumbled something Carmel didn't catch, then hastily withdrew himself to the side of the bar where Sid was beckoning.

Carmel looked down at the cheery oversized Christmas mug handed to her, then up at her friend who wore a frown on her face. "It's not what you think," she began.

"Oh I doubt that," Bridget replied shortly. An uncomfortable silence grew. Both sets of eyes followed Phonse meandering his way over to where Peters was still holding forth, haranguing the knot of men around him. The tension was rising everywhere in the room. The crowd was growing angry, with mutters and rustles coming from all sides. Even Sid at the bar looked a little perturbed. The air was thick and heavy in the enclosed space.

"It's a done deal," the hefty man's voice had grown louder as the beer flowed, rising over the music. "You can work with me or against. The heavy machinery's coming in, and the land'll be mine within the week. And don't even think of sabotaging the equipment." He further admonished them, sneering and slurring his words at the same time. It was not a pretty sight. "Cause then you'll never get your road fixed. The government giveth and the government taketh away." He grinned at his captive audience. "And my brother is the premier, so he can do what he wants. And screw all you plebes!" Peters was practically screaming by this time, his face was deep red against the pristine white of his suit as he waggled his finger in the air.

"That's enough, Peters," a deep voice cut through the air from the bar. "You're not welcome here."

At a curt nod from Sid at the bar, Phonse and another man grasped a thick arm each and made short work of marching Peters to the side door and thrusting him outside into the night. Carmel could see the large man fall heavily to his knees amid the cigarette butts on the ground. Before the old wooden door banged shut, one of the bikers heaved a leather briefcase out after him. Peters could still be heard outside through the open windows cursing the cove and all its inhabitants. Sid turned the music up a notch to drown out the voice, and the players returned to their game of pool. The bikers in the corner shook their heads disgustedly.

Phonse joined the two women again, but only for a moment. He took one last swig from his tankard, set it down on the bar and turned away.

"Where you going?" Bridget called to him over the music.

"Just... just unfinished business to clue up," he threw back over his shoulder, his face still thunderous and flushed and he walked down the aisle to the door.

The women watched as he slammed the door behind him.

"I don't like this," Bridget said in a low voice. "He's going to get himself in trouble again."

"He's very... tempestuous, isn't he?"

"He's drunk, is what he is."

Carmel deflated just a little. "Oh."

"I think he likes you, you know," Bridget continued, in a warning tone. "He was definitely giving you the eye."

Here it comes, thought Carmel. So much for the new friendship. She decided to play dumb. "But... you two... I thought you were close..."

"Close?" Bridget barked. "Of course we're close." Her eyes met Carmel's, and she suddenly laughed as

Carmel's meaning became clear. "Oh my God," she said. "No, gross!"

Eyes widening, she caught herself. "I mean, no! We're cousins, for God's sake. He used to babysit me."

The light dawned in Carmel's mind. Ah, a family relationship only, that explained the familiarity between the two. Her path could be clear. A small smile formed on her face, which her friend did not miss.

"If you like his type, that is," Bridget continued, slowly. "He's a great guy, but..."

"He's gorgeous," agreed Carmel, nodding her head with enthusiasm. "I can't believe a guy like that is single."

"Huh," Bridget replied doubtfully. "He's a little old-fashioned, though. I wouldn't have thought you went for the ... traditional kind of guy."

"Are you kidding me?" Carmel asked her. *This is getting better and better,* she thought as a feeling of joy spilled over her heart. "I didn't think there were guys like that around anymore. Tell me more."

"I may not be expressing it quite right, God forgive me." Bridget sat in thought for a second, then tried again. "You're a sophisticated woman, right? I mean, you travel the world."

"Yeah, maybe," Carmel replied, not seeing the angle Bridget was taking.

"Well, he doesn't."

"But neither do you."

"He's a fisherman," Bridget said as if that were explanation enough.

"It's an honest living."

"He lives with his mother."

"When you get to be our age," she loftily informed Bridget. "That's a sign of a good man. He's caring."

"You haven't met Aunt Vee yet." Bridget changed tack and tried again. "Did you ever hear the joke about what a Newfoundland man and Jesus have in common?"

"No, tell me," Carmel said.

"He still lives at home, has a dozen good drinking buddies, never held a steady job and his mother thinks he's God."

She saw the blank look in Carmel's eyes and shook her head. "You still don't get it, do you?" She shrugged and sighed. "I give up."

The church door was flung open, interrupting further explanation from Bridget.

"Storm's coming!" Clyde roared out as he strode through the door, minus his black satanic sidekick. His shirt was spotted with wet drops. "The wind's up, the rain's starting and it's going to be a big one."

The two women left the bar together. The weather had turned about during the time that Carmel had been inside the bar. Large drops of water hit with force, stinging her unprotected back and shoulders.

"If you have any problems with the storm," Bridget shouted as she ran across the road to her house, her words almost taken by the wind. "Call me!"

"I'll be fine!" Carmel yelled back with a grin, her heart light as she danced up the steps. The rain was washing over her hair and white dress, but she hardly noticed. She looked down towards the cove and wharf, and could see, although the rain was like a curtain now, a single light rippling down by the wharf outside Phonse's cottage. *He likes me,* she thought. She imagined his arms—oh those strong arms!—embracing her, his blue eyes, even the smell of him.

"He likes me," she whispered into the rain. It had been too long.

She dreamed that night, when she could sleep through the noise of the storm, of being out on the Tickle with Phonse in his small boat. What started as a pleasant day trip soon turned into a ride from hell, being tossed by the stormy waves, the sky black with clouds and rain lashing down. Bell Island was nowhere in sight, and soon the cove of St. Jude Without was also lost from view. Like the weather all around them, the dream-Phonse grew and stormed and raged. He sprouted a wide brimmed hat with a feather and waved his sword, and only then did she notice the Jolly Roger flying from the mast. Then he was telling her he needed to throw the ballast off board or the boat would sink, and she found herself hurled over the side and hitting the water with a splash.

Carmel woke up shivering in the gloomy morning. The dream clung to her—she could still hear the wind in her mind, feel the pitch of the small boat in the waves, and the water from the storm still dripped from her hair and down her nose.

Wait, she thought, trying to sort out all the sensations. *It was a dream, that was all, just a dream.*

"Why am I still wet then?" she asked herself, the horror of realization dawning. And was answered by the ping of water drops falling onto the iron railings of her headboard. Carmel leaped out of bed and looked above for the source of the water. Uh oh. A definite leak in the roof, and a big one. She quickly moved the bed out of harm's way and placed a small garbage bucket under the drips to catch most of the water.

Over coffee, she comforted herself with the thought that at least the dream hadn't been a premonition of yet another failed relationship in her life. She'd dreamed about the storm because of the leak. Mmm, perhaps she could get Phonse to fix the leak. She pictured his strong back (of course he would have stripped off his shirt) working away on her roof in the hot sun, and the light in his eyes as she brought him an iced lemonade... well, maybe a beer, he seemed to like his ales. Anyway, he would be hammering away on the hot tiled roof, the sweat glistening from his naked back.

She was taken from this delightful daydream by a demanding yowl at the closed window.

"Hullo, Hank," she said, opening the window. She touched the white-streaked nose through the screen.

"You stayed inside out of the storm, then," she noted, as his fur was gleaming perfection. His claw dug into her finger despite the screen.

"Ouch!" she cried. "What did you do that for?"

In answer, he jumped back down onto the porch, then yowled again out of sight.

"I'm not following you this time, stupid cat," she grumbled at him, ignoring his further protestations. Although the rain had stopped some time ago, the grass and bushes were still shiny with rain, and besides the rotten creature had just drawn blood.

When the sun finally came out, Carmel fixed herself nicely, thinking there was no better time to visit Phonse to ask him if he could help her with the roof. She smiled to herself. How timely. So it was a bit obvious, but he was a traditional kind of guy, right? A little encouragement would never hurt.

Before she crossed the road, she looked around the cove and noticed that Peters' SUV was still parked across from the church. She hadn't noticed it when leaving, focused as they were on getting home out of the lashing rain.

Odd, she thought. *He must have phoned for a ride to pick him up as he was so drunk last night. I wouldn't have taken him to be so law-abiding.* She dismissed Eric Peters from her mind as she turned with anticipation to walk down the lane towards Phonse's house.

Perhaps the heels were not such a good choice for walking on this unpaved road, she thought, wincing as she wrenched her ankle in its dainty sandal on a pothole. *But hell, my legs look fabulous,* she reminded herself, gritting her teeth.

There was an old, large and much-dented white truck in the driveway, the top washed clean from the rain. Carmel hesitated. She wondered if it wasn't too early in the day, and had almost convinced herself to turn back when a voice hailed her.

"Whatta ya want?" A heavy-set woman was hanging clothes on a line, plastic curlers in her gray hair. A line of jeans, white underwear and t-shirts danced in the warm sea breeze. She continued to pin up another t-shirt while glaring suspiciously over the clothes line. Carmel stared back in consternation.

The woman looked her up and down, noting the pretty dress and sandals, and let a malicious cackle out of her maw.

"He's not here, my dear. Try the boat," she said. "Now then, Ida, what do you think of that? Throwing herself at the poor lad. He's had enough of those sluts from away."

Another woman a yard away was also hanging clothes on a line. Similarly heavy-set, also with rollers in her hair, she could have been the first one's twin. The two tut-tutted and muttered and raised their voices in malicious glee like banshees on this bright beautiful morning.

Carmel, her face burning red, picked her way through the meadow towards the shoreline. She paused to take off her sandals, then limped her way over the boulders and down the rocky beach to the wharf. The mocking laughter still echoed in the air and her ears burned with embarrassment. On the small wharf, she shouted Phonse's name, but there was no reply.

The boat was small, just large enough to have a deck and a tiny cabin for shelter from the weather. It had been painted recently, the white glowing in the fresh morning sunshine. The name 'Ms. Vee' adorned the side in deep red with fanciful curlicues surrounding the lettering.

She climbed warily onto the boat, avoiding the fast drying puddles from last night's rainstorm on the deck. A quick peek into the door of the boat's cabin showed nothing except the usual paraphernalia of a boat, things scattered around, and not shipshape at all. A large black raincoat hung on a hook, the floorboards beneath it shiny with water, and a pair of sunglasses rested by what must be the dashboard, but boat people probably had another name for it. No sign of life here, though.

There was no way in hell she was going to walk by the house again to be mocked by that horrible old bag and her crony. Could she be the Ms. Vee honoured by the boat? The mother he lived with and who thought he was God, according to Bridget. Looking up the rocky chasm toward the bridge, Carmel drew a deep breath and made up her mind. She was going to scale the path to the road above. Anything to avoid another bout of that woman's scorn.

Clambering up the slippery path to the side, Carmel looked back down into the cold depths of the gorge. Water from last night's heavy rainfall was rushing down through the gully. The rocks themselves were washed clean, but around the banks of the gorge, human detritus was in evidence, with a rusty unclaimed bike wheel and the ubiquitous beer cans scattered under bushes. Beneath her feet, a single yellow household glove shone amid broken glass, still glittering with water from the previous night's deluge. This was not going to be an easy climb in her bare feet, but the sandals were useless on this terrain.

Steadying herself on a rocky outcrop three quarters of the way up, she happened to look down at the torrent. She suddenly understood why Peters had not driven his car home last night, for he was lying face down amid the jagged rocks below, his once white suit now sodden and tinged with rust. Even from here, he looked very dead.

Chapter 4

It seemed to take ages for the appearance of the first official vehicle, but couldn't have been more than twenty minutes. *Not bad for such an isolated spot far out of town*, Carmel thought in the corner of her mind not sunken in shock. Soon the road was blocked with cars, vans and flashing lights. The area swarmed with uniforms like a bee hive, each body pursuing its own allotted task.

Too dazed to make it back up the hill to her home after calling 9-1-1, Carmel sat on one of the large boulders strewn along the side of the road with her back to the gorge, and waited. Surprised that she could even have made a cell phone call here in the gorge, surrounded by rock as she was, she used the time to replace her sandals and nurse her paining ankle. She had wrenched it worse than she'd thought going down the rutted gravel lane to Phonse's house.

"You're the lady who made the call?" A man had materialized before her. Carmel looked up at him. He stood perhaps a couple of inches taller than her, his brown eyes carefully taking her in. A kind face, if a bit weathered, he was probably in his mid forties. He wore no uniform, but carried an air of authority all about him. There was a soft burr in his voice, a foreignness. A Scots accent.

"Yes," she said. "Is he...?" she asked although she knew the answer. No one could lie that still in a rocky gorge running with water and still be alive. She'd never seen a dead person before, except laid out in a coffin, and those corpses had been made up to look like they were merely sleeping, having a restful repose. She was not used to seeing the violence of unexpected and untimely death.

"Deceased," the man agreed. "Inspector John Darrow," he said by way of introduction. His accent was particularly noticeable on the *r* sounds.

"Carmel McAlistair," she responded automatically.

"Do you know the man?" he asked, head nodding towards the bridge and past, where Peters lay.

She nodded. "It's Eric Peters," she said. "They say he's the brother of the premier."

Darrow's eyes widened almost imperceptibly, then his face closed up, leaving only blankness. "Are you certain of that?" he asked carefully.

"Looks like his suit," she said hesitating. "And his SUV is still parked up there; you couldn't have missed it." Carmel nodded her head in the direction of the church.

"Thank you," he replied, swiftly turning away. He began to bark a series of orders to the team around him, and punched in a number on his cell. He paused to look back at her for a moment.

"You live around here?" he asked.

She found herself nodding again.

"It's alright, Inspector," she heard a familiar voice say. "I'll take her back to her house at the top of the rise, there."

"I'll be up later to speak with you." Darrow nodded his dismissal and turned back to his phone.

"Oh, Bridget!" she cried at the sight of the woman with the hennaed hair. Carmel pointed over the bridge. "Do you know...?"

Bridget nodded while firmly leading her up to her house. "Let's get a cup of tea in you," she said. "Then you can tell me all about it."

She looked down at Carmel's feet as she saw her limping up the road.

"Oh, take those stupid things off; you'll fall and hurt yourself," she said. "What are you doing with those on, around these roads?"

"Too late. I already did the damage." Carmel grimaced, but stooped to remove the foolish footwear anyway. She tried to explain. "I have a leak in the roof, and I went to talk with Phonse. It's a gorgeous day, and these match my dress, so…"

Bridget rolled her eyes. "Oh, for the love of God," she said, in a defeated tone. "If that's the worst that happens, count yourself lucky."

She said no more on the matter. Once at the house and ensconced at either end of the large red sofa, Carmel nursed her ankle while they discussed what happened to Peters over tea and a tin of shortbread cookies.

"Peters was really drunk last night," Carmel noted. "He must have fallen off the bridge and onto the rocks below." She shivered at the thought of the jagged tearing stones.

"Not a pretty way to go," Bridget said. "I wonder if he drowned or broke his neck."

"But what was he doing down that way?" Carmel wondered aloud. "His car was parked up by Sid's. And…" She stopped, aghast at the thought which came into her mind. People had been pretty angry with the man last night. Was it possible he'd been pushed over the bridge to his death? She shook her head to remove that idea. Ridiculous. Wasn't it?

"And what?" Bridget asked, watching her closely.

They were interrupted by a light knock on the front door. Carmel answered the door to the Inspector.

"Ms. McAlistair," he said. She nodded, and opened the door for him to enter.

She offered tea from the pot brewed recently, but he declined.

"I'm sure you need to talk with her alone," said Bridget, a worried look on her face. "I'll go on, then."

He stopped her before she reached the door.

"Ms. Ryan, I'd appreciate if you didn't go too far," he said. "We'll have some inquiries."

Bridget darted a silent, frantic plea to Carmel before she rushed out the door.

"What was all that about?" Carmel demanded. "What inquiries?"

"Ms. McAlistair," he began.

"Oh please, stop with the Ms.," she said. "Just call me Carmel."

"Carmel," he said, his eyes crinkling unexpectedly. "Like sweet toffee?"

"No, that's caramel," she began, annoyance rising at the memory of childhood taunting, then held herself back when she realized he was teasing. She led him into the front room.

He looked around her home, his eye resting on the large artwork over the fireplace. Her paintings were almost the only items she'd unpacked so far except for the coffee maker and some baking supplies. She loved her art—each image held a story whether it had been a gift from the creator or, like the piece with pride of place over the mantel, a work she'd fallen in love with while passing the gallery window. The gallery owner had recognized a fellow aficionado and had kindly allowed her several months to pay off the hefty price before bringing it home.

"Damian Bourke?" he asked, recognizing the artist's work as he stood up to inspect the piece more thoroughly. He leaned close and reached out his hand but did not attempt to touch the work. His fingers traced the line of the harbour and cliffs in the painting.

"You recognize his work?" Carmel was surprised that a police officer would be familiar with this obscure artist. "I'd never heard of him before I saw this piece."

"I ran across him when he stayed in the artist's residence in Pouch Cove some years ago," he admitted. He turned his warm brown eyes on her, and she found herself telling the story of how she'd acquired the painting. He was surprisingly easy to talk to for a police officer, not intimidating at all.

"Are you in the process of moving in, or out?" he asked, indicating the unpacked boxes strewn around the room.

"I just moved into the house," she said. "Amazing, isn't it? Everything I was looking for—ocean view, small community, and the right price."

She looked ruefully around at the wallpaper and water stains around the old windows. "Perhaps I should have included 'in good condition' with my request to the universe. I was awakened this morning by a leak from the roof."

He looked about the room sceptically. "The place doesn't look to be in good shape. You'll need to get that seen to before the winter," he agreed. "The salt air takes its toll on wood pretty quickly."

"The landlord did say I was to arrange for any repairs," Carmel said. "I didn't realized how much needed to be done."

"These things take time," he said. "Get the most important things seen to first. But I'd advise you to get a reputable company to do the work. Don't rely on the 'do-it-yourself' cowboys around here—you'll only be sorry in the end."

Carmel thought back to her daydream of Phonse on her roof in the hot sun.

"Mmmm," she replied noncommittally. "Yes, I'll see about that."

"And this is someone in your family?" he asked, as he stopped before a photo in a carved teak frame. Ruscan. One of the few photos she had of him, taken with a borrowed camera as a joke, because he was so averse to being caught on film. It was during their vacation to the Philippines, on the ferry crossing from Cebu to Mindanao, shortly before his disappearance. His startled gray eyes looked out at her. Was there a sign of foreboding in that face, so rarely serious, or was this her imagination, over-examining everything in hindsight? With a start, she realized she hadn't thought of him in a couple of days, not since she'd placed the photo on the fireplace mantle.

"Someone I used to know," she replied, wondering with a part of her mind if that had, in fact, ever been true.

"Tell me, why the inquiries?" she asked to change the subject. "Peters was drunk, and fell down the gorge. There were two dozen witnesses to the state he was in last night."

His thick eyebrows perked up. "And where might this large gathering have been?" he asked.

"At the church—Sid's bar next door," Carmel replied, nodding her head in that direction.

"Hmm, yes, that bar."

"He was in there before…" She caught herself just in time. No need to bring up any unpleasantness that had happened. After all, the man was dead, and why malign him further?… "before the storm."

Darrow was silent for a moment.

"Did you have any dealings with the man?" he asked.

"Only what I saw over the past couple of nights at the bar," she said. "I've never met him."

"And what was your impression of him?" the Inspector asked.

"He wasn't overly pleasant," Carmel admitted, giving a mental shrug. That wasn't speaking ill of the dead, was it? Simply the truth as she'd experienced it.

"How did he get on with others around here? Was he popular with the locals?" the man asked, his now shrewd eyes focused on her.

Peters wasn't popular. Hated might be a better word.

"Hardly," she said. "A lot of people around here seem to have threatened him at some point in the past day or so. But he was drunk and obnoxious, and deserved it. Believe me, he wasn't looking to make friends."

"His SUV was parked up by the pub," he said slowly. "What do you think he was doing down by the bridge?"

Carmel thought for a moment, then shook her head.

"Perhaps he knew he had to walk off the booze before he drove back to town," she said. "He certainly wasn't fit to drive."

Darrow nodded slowly.

"Do you think he was meeting someone?" he asked.

"I doubt that," she said, remembering back. "He'd just insulted the whole community while at the bar. I think most people around here would sooner spit on him than talk to him."

He drew a deep breath, his watchful eyes trained on her.

"I'm going to tell you, as it'll be all over the news shortly, given his brother's prominent position in politics," he began. "It wasn't the fall that killed Mr. Peters. His throat was slit with a knife."

Carmel stared at him, her mouth open but unable to form a word. She realized that the dead man's suit had been stained by blood, but she'd assumed it came from the natural injuries which would've come from a fall off a bridge onto the jagged rocks below. She shuddered as she remembered Peters' lifeless body splayed on the rocks.

"Oh, my God," she said.

"Now," the Inspector continued, "do you want to tell me more about how everyone here had something against him?"

Her mind raced around the unspoken word. Murder. What had Phonse's temper gotten him into?

"It was the development," she found herself babbling in an effort to lead the inquiry away from specific people's actions. "No one who lives here wants to see that go ahead. And he was so horrible! He swaggered in, throwing his weight around. Everyone knew it was wrong for him to get hold of the land up there, just because he's the brother of the premier."

Darrow nodded slowly. "Ah, there's the rub," he said softly, as if thinking aloud. "Premier Peters is none too popular these days with pushing through the development of the Great River in Labrador, and has had threats made against him and his family. Is this related?"

His brilliant brown eyes looked up suddenly, focused on Carmel. She felt he could see right into her mind.

"Nevertheless," he continued, the strong Scottish burr coming through, "we have to explore every possible line of inquiry."

"When did it happen?" she asked. "Or can you tell?"

He thought for a moment.

"The rain started around 10 p.m.," he said. "The doctor estimates shortly after that. We found his briefcase nearby. The rock under the case was still dry enough, though the leather was sodden."

A young female constable knocked lightly on the front door, then let herself in and joined them in the parlour.

"Ah, Constable Wright," he said, then looked over at Carmel. "You don't mind if we...?"

Carmel shook her head as the constable perched on a small chair by the door and held her notebook and pen at hand. It was dawning on her that this was now an inquiry into a murder, serious business. A man had died a very nasty death at the hands of someone who'd been in the cove last night. Her cove.

"I'll start with this morning," Inspector Darrow began. "What led you down to the bridge?"

"I was out for a walk," she said hesitantly, and saw his gaze drop to her muddied feet and the fancy sandals lying next to her.

His expressive eyebrows rose. "Down the road...The body wasn't visible from the road," he reminded her. "He'd fallen behind one of the larger outcroppings."

"Well," she went on, feeling the heat rising in her cheeks. Oh, this was embarrassing. "Yes, I was out for a walk, but I was coming up the side of the ravine from the wharf. I'd dropped down there... to see if there was any fish for sale."

He let that go for the moment, not even allowing his eyes to stray back to the strappy sandals.

"I saw Mr. Peters there, he was obviously..." she couldn't say the word.

"Dead," Darrow supplied for her.

"Yes," she said and took a deep breath. "He was dead. I scrambled up the side of the gorge and called the emergency line."

"Did you touch the body, or go near him?" he asked.

"No!" she exclaimed. "I had already turned my ankle; it was hard enough going without trying to scramble over those rocks." She pointed to her ankle, now slightly swollen under the ice pack.

"And last night?" he pressed on, no sympathy in his hard gaze. "What did you witness at the bar?"

She could hear the constable scribbling furiously behind her.

Carmel took a deep breath. How could she tell him what had happened at the bar? For two nights running, Phonse had fought with Peters after many words had passed between the two. First he'd punched him in the nose, then the next night he'd thrown Peters bodily out of the bar. That showed terrific strength and a terrible temper besides. Anything she said was going to incriminate that gorgeous man—who liked her, a little voice in her head reminded her. *But the Inspector was going to find out all this anyway*, she told herself. It looked bad for Phonse, but surely he couldn't have done the deed. If he was innocent, the police would soon see that in the course of their investigation.

So she told him, even though her heart sank with every word. Hearing the passing of events out loud, she understood that the facts inevitably pointed to her would-be lover as the culprit.

"So he was murdered." Bridget looked at Carmel, a blank expression on her white, drawn face. She didn't seem too surprised. She munched on the cookies still left from the morning.

Did this woman ever stop eating? Carmel wondered as she nodded. "The Inspector said it could be political," she said, in a weak attempt to offer comfort. "They'll be looking into all avenues. It could have been anyone, not necessarily someone from the cove."

Bridget wore a dress of a drab washed-out peach hue today, a colour which did nothing to emphasize her green eyes and caused her hennaed hair seem false and lifeless. She sat glumly on the veranda with Carmel, staring down at the paint-chipped boards beneath her bare feet. She did not appear comforted.

"And you told him," she said. "About last night."

Carmel thought that was unfair.

"I had to," she replied. "I mean, it was the truth. And I'm sure someone else would have eventually, and how would that have looked if I lied to the police?"

Bridget lifted her head and glared at Carmel.

"You don't understand," she began. "You're not from here. You couldn't possibly know."

"Know what?" Carmel shot back at her, exasperated.

"We look after each other here in the cove," Bridget said, lowering her head to examine a rotten bit of the weathered boards. She poked at it with her toe. "And Phonse, well…"

"What about Phonse?" Carmel asked, dreading to hear.

"He's… let's say, he's acquainted with the police, already," Bridget said. She saw the expression on Carmel's face and gave her a small smile and shook her head. "Oh, nothing violent, nothing really bad. One or two charges in the past. And maybe a little extra-curricular activity with his boat? The cops probably know all about it already, but he's so small time they wouldn't bother him. It's not as if he's involved with the Mafia or bike gangs or anything. He just imported enough for him and his friends."

"Are you talking smuggling?" Carmel asked. She wasn't quite sure she was hearing correctly. "Like, what? The beer in Sid's bar?"

Bridget nodded, her shoulders relaxing as if relieved to have cleared the air. "In the past, he might have done, yeah." She shrugged and continued, "Not a big deal, but it's a mark against him in the eyes of the cops."

"Have they, you know, taken him in?" Carmel asked.

Her friend shook her head.

"No, not yet," she sighed, and looked blearily out over the cove. "Not yet."

Of course, the TV crews from both local stations came out in force in time to provide live coverage for the evening news. The murder of the premier's brother was too hot a scoop to miss. They set up down by the bridge, the narrow road blocked by their vans with wires running everywhere. A shortish man in his late thirties, running to plumpness and recognizable to all viewers by his boyish good looks, large head and bowtie, stood framed by the entrance to Clyde's farm while he excitedly gesticulated for his camera. The second crew, led by a willowy ice blonde maneuvered the scenic shot overlooking the gorge and its ragged rocks below, while she looked mournfully out to sea.

The old wooden screen door slammed behind Carmel as she handed her friend a frosty German beer. She flipped off the cap of her own and swallowed the first mouthful. The sun was fast heading to the horizon on this late August afternoon. By now, Eric Peters had been dead, according to the police's rough estimates, between sixteen and twenty hours.

"And so the circus begins," Bridget said, watching the crews below.

"Have you talked to Phonse yet?" Carmel asked. "What does he have to say?"

Bridget rolled her eyes and blew the air our between her pursed lips. "Oh, believe me, I've asked," she replied. "I ran down there as soon as I left you with that cop."

"And?" she pressed. "What did he say about it all?"

Bridget gave a shrug as her answer. *Really*, thought the frustrated Carmel, *she could be a bit more explanatory.* "How did he seem?" she urged again.

"He didn't say anything," Bridget said. "He just looked at me and shook his head." She looked up at her friend with pleading in her eyes. "It's not like him," she almost whispered. "You know we're so close, we can tell each other anything. He just said... nothing. I'm scared for him this time, I really am."

Carmel thought again of the man she was feeling that insane attraction for, the almost teenage-like crush. His face was an open book. Tempestuous, yes, and impulsive, she already knew. It had probably gotten him into a lot of trouble over the years, and no doubt the fight with Eric Peters was not the first bar-room brawl he'd been in—not by a long shot. But murder? She shook her head silently. The two women again sank deep into thought. It didn't look good for Phonse.

"And here you are Bridget!" said Roxanne, cheerfully greeting them like old friends, breaking them out of their reveries.

The English woman plonked herself down between the two, an air of satisfaction emanating from her. Carmel sighed and stirred herself, giving the newcomer a hard stare as she rose to offer Roxanne something to drink. Did the woman have no feeling for atmosphere? Could she not see that the two of them were in no mood for her Girl Scout cheeriness? She'd been wondering why Bridget had been avoiding the anthropologist, but was now beginning to understand.

By the time she returned to the veranda, Bridget had told Roxanne the news of Eric Peters' death.

The Englishwoman paused to think about it.

"Forgive me for talking ill of the dead, but I had the impression Peters was none too popular around here," she said with an inquiring look.

Bridget and Carmel shared a glance and nodded.

"Yeah, he had plans for the cove that didn't include any of the residents, apparently," Carmel began.

"He was despicable," Bridget blurted out, a look of loathing crossing her face.

"But still," Carmel cautioned. "Murder? Who would do that?"

"Didn't I see you speaking with him last night?" Bridget asked, turning to Roxanne. "I don't suppose he gave any clue as to who might have hated him enough to kill him?" This last was said in a hopeful tone.

"He was drunk, and coming on to me," Roxanne said dismissively. "I found him abhorrent."

"Everyone seemed to resent this development he was proposing," Carmel said. "Everyone had a reason not to want it put in. Not to mention, he didn't make himself popular with his attitude."

'Ah, yes," replied Roxanne, sitting back in her chair. "The fairy grove."

"You mean the graveyard?" Carmel asked. "Well, yes, that would have been disturbed, too. Which I think is illegal, anyway, to plow over old graves, but I get the impression Peters wouldn't have been too bothered about that."

"The local legends are that there are fairies in the woods," Roxanne said, staying on her subject. She turned to Bridget. "How about you? Have you ever seen fairies up there?"

Bridget had remained silent, but finally spoke up.

"There's old stories," she said in a reluctant tone. "But really? In this day and age?"

Carmel smiled impatiently and brought the subject back to what was foremost on her and Bridget's minds.

"The Inspector did say it could have been politically motivated," she said. "The murder, I mean."

Roxanne stared at her.

"The Inspector? The handsome one?" she said. "Are you close with him then?"

Carmel would not have called Darrow handsome, or even particularly good-looking. His face was too squished to be considered attractive, to her mind. And he had brown eyes—not blue like, for instance, Phonse.

"No," she said. "He just mentioned it in passing."

"I'm interested," Roxanne replied, casually, perhaps just politely. "What else did he mention? Do they have any leads?"

Carmel glanced over at Bridget, who met her eyes and sighed.

"They know that Phonse and Peters didn't get along," Carmel said. "That Phonse may have, you know…"

"No," replied Roxanne, her eyes widening behind her glasses. "No, I don't know. What may Phonse have done?"

Carmel remembered that the woman had not been present in the bar the first night, and had left the building early on the second.

"Not *may* have, he *did*, alright?" burst out Bridget. "Let's not beat around the bush. He did get into a racket with Peters, both nights! He *did* bloody his nose, and he *did* toss him out of Sid's."

"And so…" continued Carmel, with a glance at Bridget. "The police may think he did it."

The group was silent for a moment.

"Well, they're wrong, if that's the case," Roxanne said defiantly, the certainty in her voice growing with every word.

"Wrong?" Bridget looked up, eyes widening as she latched on to this good news. "What do you know?"

"I know Phonse couldn't have done it after he left the bar last night," Roxanne said, her eyes bright beneath her thick fringe. "Because he was with me!"

Chapter 5

Carmel stared at Roxanne, reeling a little with the impact of this news. This was Phonse's business that he had to finish? True, it meant that he had an alibi, but at what cost? She couldn't help the green envy rising in her gorge as she contemplated Roxanne, a plain Jane with her Beatles haircut and thick ankles. How could she have lured Phonse to her bed? Phonse liked Carmel, she had that on the best authority, from someone who was closest to him. How could Roxanne do this?

And, for that matter, how could Phonse?

A sound by the gate distracted the three women, and they turned as one to stare down the steps.

There stood Phonse—red around the ears, and not a little sheepish.

"Ummm, hey, ladies!" He lifted a hand, uncertain of his welcome.

Carmel glared down coldly, willing him not to come a step further.

"I, uh, I heard what you said. And I'd just like to, I mean," he said, definitely having difficulty with this. "Thanks, Roxanne, but I don't want you to, what I'm trying to say is you really don't have to…"

Carmel's heart melted despite herself. Was he saying he didn't want Roxanne to tarnish her reputation, to be forced to admit to one and all that she's a slut, or rather that she had taken him as her lover? He was a true gentleman.

Bridget rushed down by his side.

"It's wonderful news," she said, the relief on her face palpable. "The best thing that's happened all this day." She hugged him to her close and laid her cheek on his chest.

Phonse looked confused, then it dawned on him what she was talking about.

"What? You thought I'd killed him?" he asked her incredulously, holding her at arms' length. "Geez, Bridget, you know me better than that, for God's sake!"

"Of course, I know you better," she answered hot and quick. Following on the heels of her relief came anger—the easy display of emotion must be genetic. "But the cops only know one side of you, and you can bet they'd have pinned it on you to save themselves the trouble of looking elsewhere. And it would be your own fault!" Her voice was rising. "And for once, your mother can thank God for your tom-cattin' ways, I'll be sure to tell her," shouted Bridget. "It's saving you from being bunged up in jail for a change, instead of the other way round!"

"What do you know?" He was roaring at Bridget, his temper having risen as quick as hers. "What do you know about anything?"

Phonse clenched his fists, furious with his cousin, but contained himself enough to turn and stomp off down the lane towards his house. Bridget, in turn, stormed off toward her own bungalow across the road, leaving Carmel on the veranda with Roxanne.

"My, my," said the Englishwoman. "The feuding Irish." She caught Carmel's eye and clearly got the message flashed from there. The smirk faded from her face. "I'm sorry," Roxanne said and actually sounded contrite. "That was small of me. But really, the pair of them…"

Carmel allowed herself a rueful smile in answer. *Well,* she told herself, *what else was she to do?*

Throwing a jealous tantrum like a fifteen-year-old wasn't going to change anything or solve any of the problems that now faced them. Perhaps Bridget had been wrong, and perhaps Carmel's own instinct had been wrong, too. She sure wouldn't be bothered to fight for him now. Carmel made up her mind there and then to take Darrow's advice to call in a contractor about fixing the roof.

"So what do you think?" Roxanne asked her, leaning forward, hands on her thighs. Carmel found herself under a steely and intelligent gaze. She met it straight on.

"I can't believe the murderer is one of the residents of this cove," Carmel replied. "Sure, they all had reason enough to hate Peters, but kill him?" She shook her head. "No, I just can't buy that."

Roxanne leaned back with a small smile on her face.

"Not even a *crime passionel*?" she asked softly. "Hot summer night, they'd all had a few drinks. Peters acted like he was deliberately trying to rouse them."

Carmel stared at her, as Roxanne's suggestion tickled something in her mind. The thing that had been niggling her about this whole business finally began to jell and become clear.

"But that's it!" she exclaimed, jumping up as the thought hit her. "Maybe this wasn't a spur of the moment murder stemming from a drunken fight."

She looked at Roxanne, who stared back apprehensively, then Carmel lowered herself back into the chair.

"You see," she explained in a gentler tone to the the Roxanne. "You left before the storm broke. The rain was just starting when we all cleared out of the church last night."

Roxanne nodded slowly. "Okay, but I fail to see what you're getting at," she said.

"It was pouring out there," Carmel said, feeling the smug rush of triumph that happens when neurons are making connections. "Everyone was scurrying for cover. In fact, Bridget and I didn't even notice Peters' SUV was still there, and we had to have splashed right by it. No one local was going to be hanging around getting into fights."

Roxanne looked relieved at this explanation. "Yes, I see your point," she said. "Too wet for emotions to be running high, you're saying."

"Precisely," Carmel said, and leaned back into her chair. "Maybe it was an outside job—one that was planned ahead of time. It just so happened that the murderer was lucky enough to have the rain on their side. He was able to do this terrible thing under cover of the storm, and get away with it, because anyone else out on the road would be scurrying to get out of the weather." She was satisfied with this explanation as far as it went, but conscious that there was something still missing from the picture. It would come to her eventually—these things did—so she let it go. She had a good working hypothesis, and she was going to stick with it for now.

Carmel found herself feeling much warmer towards the Englishwoman now, despite whatever had passed between her and Phonse the night before. The other woman was a little odd at times, yes, but she offered a sensible, unemotional sounding board for Carmel's thoughts.

"The fact that Peters had his throat slit…" Roxanne began, speaking slowly as if in thought.

Carmel waited for her to finish.

"Throat cutting has been a method of ritual killing in many cultures in the past," she continued. "Take for example, the ancient Aztecs and their human sacrifices.

Their stone altars had special channels carved in to collect the blood, and it's a common theme in their art."

"I don't think this was a ritual sacrifice," Carmel replied. "Not along the lines you're talking about. His blood wasn't collected in a bowl, not that we know of."

"No, perhaps you're right. But there have been other groups who've espoused the slit throat as a method of punishment," Roxanne continued. "I don't suppose Peters was of the Mormon persuasion, was he?"

Carmel shook her head. "Doubt it. I gather he worshipped Mammon and money more than God."

"Pity. Mormons used to have a penalty on their books. Let's see, it went, 'My throat... be cut from ear to ear, et cetera...'" if they spoke of their secret initiation ceremonies. But that's been stricken now, at any rate, so that wouldn't fit."

"I don't think there's a religious element in this," Carmel answered.

"No, you're right," the other said. "Perhaps we're dealing with a run-of-the-mill Jack the Ripper type of murderer." She glanced over to the other. "You're not keen on that idea either, eh? Ah well, Peters was hardly a prostitute in Victorian London."

Carmel was wishing Roxanne wasn't quite so informed about the why's and how's of human murderous tendencies throughout the ages. It was bad enough having a murder occur down the road from her home without introducing the idea of a serial killer on the loose. She shivered as she looked about the peaceful-seeming cove and decided to change the subject.

"So you're an anthropologist. What's your area of specialty?" Carmel asked, partly out of true curiosity. She loved to hear about what drove other people, as a true passion can make any subject fascinating.

"Oh, you'll laugh," Roxanne replied, looking almost shy.

"No, I won't," Carmel said.

"Fairies," the other woman said. "I document folklore fairies around the world."

Carmel blinked. This sturdy woman, who looked as if her feet were firmly planted on the ground, spent her life studying fairies? Absurd.

"Well, I guess this is a good place for you to be then," she said. "The old woman through the woods can give you an earful about that."

"You've met her then?" Roxanne asked. "She's spoken with you about the legends?"

Carmel paused to consider, then shook her head.

"Just in passing," she said. "Melba seems a little loopy, quite honestly. I don't think you'll get a straight story out of her."

"Oh," said Roxanne, disappointment on her face. "I had been really hoping…"

"So you're here doing research, then?"

"Pure coincidence," Roxanne said, and she gave a rueful laugh. "You know how it is if you're focused on one thing, any hint of it will catch your attention. Turns out to be a busman's holiday, really." She looked down at her watch. "Look at the time," she said, and quickly made her good-byes.

Carmel watched Roxanne make her way down the lane to the small cottage on the point. All this talk of ritual murders had unsettled her, she had to admit. And then there was Melba, with her biblical sounding talk as she had cursed Peters the other day. The woman wasn't quite right in the head. Could she have acted out her threats? *No.* Carmel firmly put this out of her mind. Stick to the theory of the outsider, not her next-door neighbour. It was far more comfortable.

Carmel finally had some time to herself after the long day, and she realized she was starving as she poked through her freezer to find something to satisfy. Living in this cove seemed to be affecting her appetite, for so much of life here revolved around food. Yes, she loved to cook and bake, just not every day. When she was in the mood, she could create with the best of them, but if not—well—her creations were indifferent at best. She was certainly too hungry to bother right now, and there was the rest of the pie to look forward to, drippy as it was.

As she munched her way through a vegetarian curry with rice, she turned the news on the TV, to see if there had been any developments. The avid face of Gerald Smythe, the boy-man newscaster, and his mustard-coloured shirt filled the screen which was perched on the kitchen counter.

"This just in! The RNC are stating there's no word yet on the gruesome murder of Eric Peters, brother of the premier." He proceeded to give the grislier details of Carmel's morning discovery. "Everyone is asking— is this a political murder? Are the island residents finally rebelling against the heavy hand of the premier?

"Now, an exclusive interview with Inspector Darrow of the Royal Newfoundland Constabulary," he continued. The shot fell back to include the Scotsman, his face tired, blinking in the brightness of the camera lights. "Inspector, what can you tell our viewers about this murder? Should they be worrying that there's a local terrorist cell operating? Or is it the action of a crazed madman?"

Darrow startled at his words. "It's not my opinion that this is terrorist action, no," he said. "The Police have begun our investigation. Other than that, I'm afraid, I can give no comment."

"No comment," Gerald repeated, in a voice laden with meaning as the camera zoomed back on him, his eyes lit with excitement. "We all know what that usually means. They haven't got the proverbial clue."

He paused as if waiting for the canned laughter, his oops-I-did-it-again smile dancing on the boyish face. "So, Inspector, what do you think the chances are you'll get your man?"

The camera again fell back, but to an empty space. A pout was evident on the news reporter's face as he watched the inspector leave off camera, quickly filled by a growing frown of spite. It was an unfortunate expression for his face, bringing his features too close together, making him look like an unlikable cartoon character. "Well, that speaks volumes," he nodded knowingly at the camera, a smile flashing on his face again, but one that didn't reach his eyes.

"For God's sake, what drivel," Carmel muttered as she switched over to the rival local station, just in time to catch the willowy blonde glumly sum up the activities on the site down the road, the setting sun catching her long blonde hair.

"...the grisly murder of a prominent city business man in a tiny community which, frankly, no-one has ever heard of before today. The police have no leads, but claim they are pursuing the political aspect." She looked disparagingly around her, the camera following, finally coming to rest on Phonse's lone boat at the old wharf, and gave a visible shiver. "Reporting live from St. Jude Without, this is Veronica Dourley," she finished as the camera framed her withering look.

Carmel switched off the news, still trying to get her head around what had happened in the cove the previous night, and her thoughts continued as she took her post-prandial cigarette on the back step. She'd found that sitting on her front veranda was taken as an invitation for any passing neighbour to join her, and she wanted time alone to sort her thoughts.

What really happened to Peters? she found herself wondering. Although she'd been sure it must have been an outside job when she was discussing the matter with Roxanne, now she wavered. True, no one would have noticed a strange car around, in all that rain last night. She and Bridget hadn't even registered Peters' large Mercedes SUV as they ran past it.

"Or at least, I didn't notice it," she said aloud. Could she speak for Bridget? What did she really know of this woman, based on a couple of days' acquaintance? She realized that Bridget had been worried the police might pin the murder on Phonse, not that Phonse may have done it. There was a world of difference between the two, and it had to be significant. Did Bridget know who the murderer was? Was it Bridget? She didn't like the path her thoughts were taking her. Sitting here, surrounded by the darkening woods, her mind was beginning to create shadows where none had been before.

Still, the quiet of the woods at dusk lulled her. The rain had washed away the mosquitoes and black flies, while the ear-splitting roar of the motorcycles was conspicuously absent that evening. Due, she suspected, to the heavy police presence still in the cove.

"Bikers," she said as the thought came to her. Bikers had been in the bar last night. Yes, she could remember them hulked into their usual corner close to the bar. Could they have taken a hit out on Peters? One of them had thrown his briefcase out after him—could another have slipped out the front and done the deed? They were a rough-looking crowd, all muscle and tattoos and hair. Maybe she could make inquiries of Sid.

Wait a moment, she caught herself. What did she know of Sid, or any of the cove people, for that matter?

He'd been over conferring with the bikers last night, his eyes shifting around the bar. She pictured the old blue tattoos running the length of his arms. Sleeved, the prison slang was for it. She realized that he, too, could be one of the bikers. *Oh dear God,* she thought to herself. *What sort of place have I moved in to?*

Lights flickering in the woods distracted her from these thoughts.

"And now fairies?" she muttered to herself, her conversation with Roxanne still fresh in her mind. Carmel watched as the flickering grew stronger, resolving itself into a single beam accompanied by the sound of breaking branches and mild oaths in the woods.

No fairy, she realized, but a man, as he stepped out of the bushes. The light shone in her face.

"Put that away, whoever you are," she said, by now much annoyed at the intrusion. Could she not get any peace in this place? Carmel had always been a loner, and part of the attraction of this isolated cove had been the quiet and lack of neighbours. She couldn't have been more wrong, she was quickly coming to realize, for there was no way one could practice being a hermit here with people in her face all the time.

"Ms. McAlistair?" a voice called out, and the light switched off.

"Carmel, please," she reminded the Inspector. He walked towards her in the twilight, brushing leaves off his white shirt. A dark tie was slung around his neck. He straightened it before presenting himself to her.

"I was hoping to find you in," he said.

"And I was hoping for a little peace," she muttered. "What can I do for you?" she continued, more politely.

"I'd like a word, if you don't mind," he replied, sitting himself beside her on the step. He smelled faintly of soap with something stronger, something darker and spicier, lurking beneath.

"Beer?" she asked him, hospitably.

He shook his head. "No, thanks, much as I'd welcome it," he said. "I'm on the job."

"I saw you on the news," she said.

"Idiots, all of them," he replied decisively. She laughed in agreement.

"So is this an official visit?" she queried. "An unorthodox approach, wouldn't you say?" She indicated the woods behind her house from which he'd emerged.

Darrow grinned, his teeth gleaming in the light of the kitchen window.

"I needed to speak with the old lady across the way, the one they call Melba," he said. "Then I thought I'd take a shortcut through the woods to your place."

He laughed and continued. "Not much of a shortcut in the dark."

"How did you find her, Melba?" Carmel asked. "I mean, her state of mind."

"She seems bright enough, and not traumatized by the whole business," he said, considering. "Of course, with all the rain last night, and her cottage being set back so far in the woods, she claims she didn't hear or see anything."

"Melba didn't seem a little, oh, not quite with it, to you?" she asked, hesitantly. "Perhaps a touch of senility?"

Darrow looked at her, surprised.

"No, I found the lady as sharp as any other around here," he said. "Perhaps sharper than some. As I said, I wanted to talk with you," he continued. "You've just moved into the cove, and you said you have no ties here? No past history?"

Carmel nodded in agreement, then shook her head.

"I mean, no," she said. "The opportunity to rent the house came up out of the blue, and I'd never even heard of St. Jude Without before this. I'd always thought the North Point Road ended in Portugal Cove."

"Strange, that," he said. "The cove manages to keep under the radar, for the most part." He glanced at his watch. "Office hours are over," he said. "Perhaps I will take you up on that beer now."

When she returned with two bottles, one for each of them, he looked appreciatively at the German labels on the bottles. Carmel wasn't much of a beer drinker, and the beer strike hadn't really affected her in any way. However, she could enjoy a cold drink on a hot day so she'd brought in a dozen beer of a German make, in really cool reusable bottles with a flip-lid attached.

"Good beer," he noted. "Glad to see it was bought legally."

Carmel laughed. "I know how faithful people are to the local beers." She paused for a moment while she sipped. Could she find out if the authorities suspected Phonse? True, he had an alibi in Roxanne, but she'd experienced enough third world country politics to know that alibis didn't always count for much, not when the police wanted to close a case quickly. And a high profile case like the murder of the premier's brother was definitely one they'd want to get off their books in a hurry. Bridget had said the cops had their eyes on Phonse—and she'd also hinted he was up to illegal activities. She took a deep breath and decided to sound him out. "With the beer strike on, I imagine there's smuggling going on?" she added in a casual tone.

He didn't give her an inch with his reply. "When is there never smuggling here?" he asked. "There's just much more happening now."

Darrow got to the point of his visit after he'd downed the first swallow. "The murder of Peters," he said. "As I said, you're an outsider, but you've met a lot of the residents of the cove. Can I ask you your ideas on the whole matter?"

So they were both fishing for information from the other. Perhaps if she played her cards right, she could gain some information and help solve this terrible mystery. This idea appealed to her—Carmel McAlistair, super-sleuth. Forgetting all about Phonse, she took a moment to gather her thoughts.

"I really don't think it could have been done by anyone living here," she said. "It occurred to me today that the rain, pelting down as it was when we left the bar last night, well, I was thinking, it would have discouraged any hot emotions from carrying over. Everyone would have been more concerned with getting out of the downpour, than stalking and murdering Peters, no matter what they had against him.

"So I think it must have been premeditated, maybe the political angle you mentioned earlier. It was the perfect opportunity for someone to commit a murder and get away with it," she finished. She sighed after she'd said that, because as an argument, it was sounding weaker every time she put her mind to it. She would really have to do better than this if she wanted to become a sleuth.

He paused in thought. "There have been one or two developments which have come to light," he said. "For one thing, we've ruled out an outside party, and thus we're no longer considering the murder a politically-motivated hit."

Carmel turned to look at him, swatting away a moth which was trying to land on her hair. It hadn't been a strong argument she'd presented, but it was worth checking into and she felt it shouldn't be dismissed out of hand. "How you can just rule it out?" she asked. "You know there's a lot of anger around the whole province about the graft and corruption coming to light from the premier's office. He's appointed his whole family in places of prominence, not to mention his friends. It's like a banana republic here, for God's sake, and people are really pissed at the whole thing. Look at what's happening on George Street every night. I'm only surprised it was his brother got himself killed, and not the premier himself."

"I'm not saying you don't have a point," he said, eyeing her with a slight smile on his face. "Never the less, we've evidence that it was someone inside the community, and I can't see any of this lot caring a hoot about the world outside their own little cove."

She held her words, knowing he was not yet finished.

"Y'see, there was a landslide in Portugal Cove last night," he said. "Right after the heavy downpour began. Mud and boulders all came down at the outcrop just south of the junction of North Point Road and the laneway to the ferry."

"But the police cars and ambulance made it through this morning just twenty minutes after I made the emergency call," she objected. "There's no way they could have cleaned up such a heavy spill so quickly. It's not like North Point Road is a major artery—it only leads to St. Jude Without."

"Ay, you're right there," he said kindly. "But any traffic in and out of the cove had to be rerouted to go down the lane and past the ferry terminal. And in doing so, it would be caught on the security cameras the Department of Transportation set up after all the fuss they had with vandalism down there last year."

She stared at him, taken aback.

"You mean to say," she said, but didn't finish as she didn't quite know what she meant to say.

"Yes, I do," he replied firmly. "There's nought could get past that narrow road without getting caught on film."

He pronounced the last word as if it had two syllables. In fact, she'd noticed, his Scottish accent was becoming stronger as the beer passed down his throat. *I quite like the sound of it,* she thought, *very comforting yet authoritative.* It was the voice of a man you'd want to have around in an emergency situation—the owner of that voice would soon take charge and sort out any messes.

But this knowledge changed things, even she had to admit, and she sat staring at the dark woods around them as she fully took in the meaning of his words. There was a murderer among them in the cove. Desperately, she grasped at a straw dangling in the corner of her mind. "The bikers," she remembered, then continued in a stronger voice. "There have been bikers hanging around the bar ever since I got here, you know." Carmel turned to look at him full on. "And they're real bikers, too," she emphasized. "Not your yuppies going out on their expensive toys on the week-end, not them. They're all hairy with tattoos, and they look nasty." They weren't local, not from the cove.

The Inspector was nodding in agreement.

"There's always that aspect," he said. "Another avenue to explore. Did you see them in the cove last night?"

She pictured them in their dark corner near the bar, Sid leaning over them, covertly glancing around him while he stroked his moustache. The sinister bar owner was mixed up with them, she realized. The bikers were his cohorts, and they were only present because of him.

"Oh, yes," she answered. "They were in the bar last night. Though whether they were all still there when we left, I couldn't tell you."

"You left before the rain began, or after?"

"It was just bursting when we went out."

"Shortly after Peters was evicted, you'd say?"

"Yes," she said. "Peters was… helped out of the side door. About fifteen or twenty minutes later, Clyde Farrell came in, and said the rain was starting, and we were just leaving then."

Darrow considered this then shook his head. "We've already ruled the bikers out. I'm fairly certain it couldn't have been one of them."

"What do you mean?" asked Carmel, becoming just a little aggrieved again. Why was he bothering to ask her opinion if he'd already examined and discarded every idea she had?

"We found the three of them camped out on the floor of the church this morning," he told her, a small smile on his face. "Their gear was bone dry, and quite frankly, none of them smelled like they've been near flowing water for a week. There's no way one of them could have been out in last night's downpour."

She stared glumly in front of her as the news sank in.

"They could have borrowed Sid's rain coat?" she asked weakly, not wanting to give up on the biker idea. Without them to hang it on, it had to be a local. Someone she'd already met, perhaps drank a beer with. Without the bikers, Carmel had possibly consorted with a murderer.

Darrow was shaking his head.

"That's not all," he said, then gave a heavy sigh. "I haven't told you all of it."

"I'm almost afraid to ask," she replied with trepidation.

"It's the murder weapon itself," he said. "We found it not far from where the body landed."

She waited, braced for the worst.

"The murder weapon was a fish-knife," he said slowly. "Or more specifically, as it's known around here—a cut-throat."

Chapter 6

After Darrow had made his departure, Carmel hurried inside to make sure all the doors were locked and windows secured throughout the house. A murderer in the cove—his words had turned her unspoken fears into reality. And the worst of it was, it could be anyone. Hard as it was to believe, any of the people she'd met could be the murderer.

He'd explained that until recent years, St. Jude Without had been, like almost every single tiny community in the province, dependent on the inshore fishery. All the family members of each household contributed to their livelihood, in salting and preparing the cod on the beaches and wooden flakes. And the fish gutting knife—or cut-throat—maybe two or three of them, would be found in every home. There might even be a couple hidden in the back of a drawer in her own kitchen. She didn't want to look. The back door was securely bolted.

Carmel made her way around the rest of the downstairs, using the overhead hall light to find her way around. She passed through the living room to check the windows there. Thinking she saw a shadow twitch, a hint of a movement in the darkened corner by the fireplace, she flicked on the overhead light and turned to face whatever awaited. But there was, of course, nothing there. Not much had changed in the room since she'd last left it, the opened boxes remained where she'd left them, with the exception of a book now laying on the coffee table. But she must have removed it from the shelf herself, and absentmindedly left it there. It was one of the few books left by her landlord Frank Ryan along with an assortment of odd dishes, and she could see the space on the shelf where it had sat.

Carmel took the book in her hand. It was an old book, its red leather binding stained and faded over the years, warm to her touch. *Pirates of the New Founde Land* was the title. She firmly returned it to the empty slot on the shelf. This was not light bedtime reading, not for a night like this.

Darrow had killed the biker theory dead, Carmel thought glumly as she made her way upstairs to bed. "They would use a more conventional weapon like a gun or a switchblade. Likewise a politically-linked assassination."

Even international terrorist activity was out of the question, too, for a would-be assassin would never make it into the country with a knife like that. Though of course, professional assassin had never been a serious contender. The murderer was someone from the cove.

Carmel still didn't have peace of mind the next morning. In fact, she'd slept very little over the long night with worrying and wondering and listening to the strange noises made by an old house settling for the night, and right now she just wanted to clear her head with fresh air and exercise. Looking around the living room with all its half-unpacked boxes, she decided to do something productive. She would take a walk into Portugal Cove to the store, and on the way would inspect the landslide for herself. The swelling in her ankle had gone down—it was just a minor sprain—and the exercise would do her good if she took it slow.

Miraculously, she made it through the whole length of St. Jude Without not passing another soul. It was far too early an hour for the media, and even the police were absent from the cove, having taken all their evidence and moved back to the comfort of their building in the city centre. Phonse's boat was gone from the wharf, though far down by his house, she could see a figure hanging out laundry to dry in the soft ocean breeze—sheets this time. *His mother*, she decided. Ms. Vee. She gave a small moue of distaste at the memory of their encounter. *Imagine having a mother-in-law like that*, Carmel thought, glad that she'd quickly gotten over that crush.

No Bridget, no Roxanne, and she was glad to enjoy the solitude of her walk. The water glinted in the Tickle, and the now-familiar toot of the ferry landing was like music to her ears. After last night's fears, she appreciated the signs of civilization. Heading south on North Point Road, she passed the first few houses in the small neighboring town.

Just past the lane which turned down to the ferry off North Point Road, Carmel saw the signs of where the landslide had been. A large boulder which had tumbled out of a precarious hillside back yard had been pushed back to the side of the road, no doubt by heavy equipment, and the pavement still showed large clumps of mud on it. She stopped and gazed at the mountain above, perilously close at this point, the road narrowly winding past. The neighbouring houses had been lucky they hadn't been in the path of the large rock slide.

It struck her that this was the explanation for all the boulders strewn along the road to her community— each one had at some time fallen from the mountain above and had been subsequently shoved out of the way and left at the side of the road, there being no more convenient place to store them. Eventually perhaps, the whole mountain would make its way down, and block off the road forever. What a dreary thought for a beautiful morning.

Rather than take the shorter road to the highway, she decided to walk by the ferry terminal to see for herself the only route available that night. A steep incline down to the large wharf and breakwater, then a long climb back up past the confusing array of lanes meant to lend an air of order to the lines of traffic waiting for the ferry at peak times. She continued on her way to the convenience store located at the turnoff from the main highway to the ferry terminal. The building was part of a mini-strip mall with a pizzeria, pub, liquor store and other businesses attached in a hodgepodge fashion, as if they had organically sprouted to fill the roadside corner. *A profitable place to have a business*, she thought, looking at the long line of cars waiting to board the morning ferry. At this time of day, they were probably mostly tourists going over to explore the old iron mines whose arms stretched way out under the sea, now made into a very secure museum. The commuters from the island would already be at their jobs in the city.

The small grocery store had a surprisingly large array of vegetables to offer, all local produce fresh from the farms at this time of year. The very talkative clerk assured her that although nothing was labeled organic, the famers hereabouts didn't use pesticides, they just didn't bother with certification as it was too expensive a procedure, flying in a specialist to certify what everyone already knew, and why couldn't the provincial government provide this service anyway, she wanted to know. It was reassuring to Carmel to experience the everyday normality of her chatter after the dark day just past in the next cove over.

There was a small coffee shop and bakery attached and the aroma was heavenly, too tempting to pass up.

She took her coffee and croissant outside to the picnic tables scattered on the grass. The table next to her was abuzz with the latest news from St. Jude Without, she couldn't help overhearing. It appeared to be an impromptu meeting of the town council over breakfast and coffee.

"As Mayor, I'm prepared to take whatever action necessary to make sure we can claim that land," one man vehemently pounded his fist on the wooden table top as he spoke. "We can't let this sort of threat happen again."

"But the crowd over to St. Jude's are not going to agree to amalgamate, Thomas Ryan, sure you knows that," one tall thin man said as he mournfully shook his head. "We've been through it all before."

The rest of the people seated murmured their agreement.

"We'll go through it again and again until they see the light," the first man argued. "We can get them on board with this plan, especially now that Peters is out of the way."

He leaned in and spoke in a lower tone, although Carmel could still make out his words. *He must think I'm a tourist passing through,* she thought, and dismissed her as a disinterested party.

"Farrell has to be on side with us now. He came that close to losing it all, that the cantankerous old bastard will have learned his lesson," he said.

"He still won't open up his land to the trail," someone pointed out.

The mayor waved his hand in dismissal.

"Doesn't matter, we can deal with that when we come to it," he said. "Besides, if we can get the land proclaimed as a Heritage site, then we can make our own trails above his farm."

From what she could gather, they appeared to be planning a coup, with the small town of Portugal Cove intent on swallowing up the tiny cove she now lived in. Carmel could hardly believe her ears at this turn of events. Turned out the council in Portugal Cove had not wanted Peters' development to happen either, as they would not be gaining any tax dollars from it. The mayor's plan of amalgamation included making the crown land in dispute into a heritage site, as the last known encampment of the Beothuk Indians in the area before Clyde Farrell's forebears had chased them off. This, he told his willing cohorts, would create yet another tourist attraction to boost the town's economy.

Carmel's good mood had deflated by the time she set off on her slow journey home, feeling her ankle throb again. Was there no end to the intrigue in this small place?

Once home, she decided it was time to get back to her writing, so she again turned her back on the mess in her living room. She hadn't checked her emails yet today. And she hadn't done a Google search for Ruscan for a few days with all the excitement in the cove.

She had set up a small home office in what had been the dining room of the old house, and it was there she now forced herself to sit. It had a window facing the road, along with another facing down the hill towards Farrell's farm. She'd just missed the arrival of the reporters, she noted as she settled herself at the writing table, for from this vantage point, she could see all around the cove. One van painted an unnatural green with the lurid red and yellow station logo plastered on its side took the optimum location down by the bridge and the scene of the crime. Gerald Smythe leaped out, a happy smile on his face as he looked around, excitedly indicating points of interest to him.

Not long after, the similarly-sized white van with a quieter paint job pulled up, hesitated at the top of the rise as if not wanting to be seen by the other crew, then retreated. By the sound of it, they pulled off to park by the church. This was Veronica's crowd

Carmel's attention was caught by more movement down by the bridge. Clyde Farrell was coming down his laneway, and she could almost see the smoke rising from his ears. This should be good. She pushed away her laptop and prepared to be entertained.

And Farrell did not disappoint. Through the open window, she could hear the altercation between Smythe and the farmer who was accompanied by his black dog on a length of heavy chain. Between the loud growls of one and the strong cursing of the other, it looked as if Smythe was not being given a chance to splash around his charm. As Clyde stalked back up the hill, clanging the gate behind him, she could see the reporter frowning and even from this distance, she could see his face screwed up with spite as he climbed back into the van. It made its way up the incline and back through the cove.

This was too good to miss, she knew, so she abandoned the pretense of writing and snuck out of her house, hiding behind the lilac bush. Peeking out around towards the church, she saw Bridget cycling up the North Point Road in her direction. Microphone in hand, Veronica Dourley, dressed in a lightweight black suit with a tiny skirt which further emphasized the unlikely length of her tanned legs, flicked her blonde locks and ignored the passing hippy-chick with the dark red hair.

Gerald Smythe, however, pounced at the sight of a likely female. He paused directly in her path, but the cheeky smile emblazoned across his face fell off into a petulant frown as Bridget darted out of his way without acknowledging him. Carmel noted, however, his blonde rival had taken this in, and was now sneering and laughing with her crew. This jeering from his rival brought on a deep flush of embarrassment on Smythe's face, and he sent a poisonous glare at Bridget's back for being the cause of it. Smythe was really not happy with his treatment by the residents of the cove.

Carmel giggled as she hobbled across the road, meeting Bridget as the other woman swung off her bike and flung it to the ground inside her gate.

"C'mon in and watch from my window," Bridget said, grabbing her arm as she drew her inside. "I have a feeling this is going to be too good to miss. My house has the better view."

Now that the shock of the murder had been absorbed, the community was coming alive again. A gaggle of young teen-age girls materialized out of their homes, enticed away from their cell phones and their computer games by the appearance of the cameras. They stood and giggled, pushing each other in the direction of Gerald Smythe, his face made famous by the evening news hour watched by their parents. He preened for them, sending them into a paroxysm of delighted shrieks as they hitched up their tiny skirts further and posed amid the roadside boulders and scrub. Ms. Dourley they merely gawked at with open mouths, unsure if she were really flesh and blood.

After a minute, there was action as the front door of the church opened for the exit of Sid and his biker friends. Despite the hot day, all four were dressed in full leathers with helmets already in place. They strode, heads down, to the bikes parked in the barren lot between the church and rock face.

Veronica threw a quick look at Gerald as if to say, 'This is how it's done.' She twisted her face into a sultry expression, and sidled off after the men, hips forward like a model on the catwalk, confident in her sex appeal. Just as she opened her deep red lips, the air filled with the ear-splitting percussion of the four Harleys and Triumphs starting their motors in tandem. The noise reverberated off the stone walls of the church, echoed from the rock face and bounced back to the church to start the cycle all over again. She winced and held her hands over her ears but pushed on nonetheless, determined to seduce a good story from these males. Each time she approached an individual and opened her mouth, all four revved their engines up twice as hard. You'd almost think they were enjoying themselves.

Finally, they tired of their game, and with engines suitably warmed, pulled out one by one onto the road and headed into town, until only Veronica's curses were heard in the small lot. The teens looked on with awe as they stored up the words which would be repeated with much bravado during the evening hang-out in front of the boys, to impress with their sophistication.

The show wasn't over quite yet. Unnoticed by all, Mrs. Ryan had made her way up from the small home she shared with her son, and stood at the top of the laneway tut-tutting about the rowdy bikers and how they were ruining this peaceful cove. Gerald Smythe, being the closer, claimed her.

"I never seen the like." She shook her head, jowls wobbling just a little. Mrs. Ryan was dressed in her Sunday best and, much as she'd sneered at Carmel's dainty sandals, had managed to struggle up the lane in her shiny court pumps—those worthy sensible heels usually reserved for the rare cove wedding. "This is the most law-abiding... well, we never had trouble before. And a murder? It had to be someone from the outside, had to be. Sure, everyone in the cove is my family, and we likes to keep ourselves to ourselves." After much more of the same, Gerald got a word in.

"An interview? Oooh I couldn't," she said. "My hair's a mess. What's that? Oh, you're a sweet man for saying so."

Her hair, finally free from the constant curlers, was more of a neatly ordered helmet of curls rather than the mess she claimed. Orangey pink lipstick outlined her mouth, while her eyes shone out from beneath the bright blue paint which had been popular in her youth. Despite her protestations, she was surprisingly ready to snatch her fifteen minutes of fame.

"Call me Vee, dear," she simpered as Gerald took her arm and firmly led her down the lane to her home, both happily on the way to achieving their aims. The heavy van followed at a snail's pace behind them as it slowly rolled its way over the ruts and gullies of the gravelled road.

Ensconced back at her desk, instead of focussing on the editing work and emails which awaited her, Camel found her mind wandering back unavoidably to the puzzle Darrow had set out last night. Someone in the cove, but who? And more to the point—why? As Sherlock or Marple or one of their ilk had said, once you know the *why,* you will know *who* dunnit. Too bad there wasn't a convenient butler in the cove to pin it on.

She set up a spreadsheet listing all the residents of the cove. Once she started thinking about it, she realized that the 'why' wasn't such a hard question to answer after all. Everybody hated Peters. Period. Nobody liked him, welcomed him or had a good word to say about him.

But hated him enough to kill him? That was another matter.

She began in no particular order. Clyde Farrell, the farmer, whose family had been here for generations. Unlike most of the island's original settlers, the Farrells were farmers more than fishermen, although she had no doubt there would be a fish-gutting knife or two to be found on his property even if they just fished for their own use.

Would Clyde have had the opportunity? By all means, the murder having happened just down the lane from his home at the end of the cove. A dark and rainy night like that, there would have been no fear of witnesses. There were no other houses down there, save Melba's cottage tucked away in the woods. Peters had been turfed out of the bar before Clyde had entered that night. There had been plenty of time for the two to meet as Clyde made his way into the cove, have an argument, and before you know it, there was Peters with his throat cut and tossed over the bridge. Clyde was a nasty man, to be sure. Her heart still raced when she thought of the dog's attack on her.

Clyde claimed that the development would ruin the water table, and the runoff from uprooting the trees would wash away the topsoil so carefully tended over the past couple of hundred years.

Yes, Clyde was on her list.

Next came Melba. Although she may or may not have been of sound mind, she was a big woman, tall with a muscular build beneath her baggy, ill-fitting clothes. Carmel had heard with her own ears the curses the old woman rained down upon Peters, and it was a terrible anger indeed that the woman had shown. She really did believe in the fairy who she claimed would give him his come-uppance, although Carmel had a hard time imagining this. *Weren't fairies lovely and blythe?* she thought, thinking of the various fairies in the tales of her childhood. Surely a graveyard would be a downer for those sprites? At any rate, by the violence of her curses against Peters, Melba had enough rage in her to do away with the man herself, with or without the help of supernatural forces. And she hadn't seemed particularly sane to Carmel, no matter what the Inspector said.

Carmel could picture the scene. The dark night, the pouring rain, Melba rushing down the path that led from her house, accosting the man, slitting his throat and heaving the dying man into the gorge below, with enough force to throw him past the jagged line of rocks. The hard rain would have quickly washed away the blood. She shivered at the thought.

So yes, Melba had to stay on the list. *Unless,* Carmel thought, *it was her curses which had done him in, bringing the wrath of her fairy friends down on the man?* That would be the perfect murder, totally unprovable as no one would believe it. She chided herself for this foolishness and went back to the task.

Thinking back on her morning visit to Portugal Cove, she added that town's mayor to the list too. Yes, it was a long shot, but she was determined to be thorough in her newfound calling of super-sleuth. The man had shown no false remorse at the news of Peters' passing, and the Portugal Cove major definitely had his own agenda in wanting to increase his town's tax base. He might even be working in cahoots with Clyde.

Lost in her reverie, Carmel failed to notice the noises outside, until a loud hammering forced her attention to the world around her. Checking both front and back doors, she could see no one, but still the banging continued. Just a little frightened but quickly becoming a whole lot annoyed, she strode out the back and looked up on the roof.

There was Phonse tearing up the tiles on the far corner of her roof, right over her bedroom. Just as she had imagined the other day, he wore no shirt, his back and chest gleaming with sweat. His cut-off jeans showed fine muscled legs, covered in golden hairs shining through the tan.

Oh, what a sight. He was a handsome one. "What are you doing up there?" she cried out, hands on her hips and trying to hold onto her annoyance. He looked down and cheerily waved a greeting.

"I remember old Uncle Frank had been complaining about the roof leak for years," he called back. "I figured he'd want me to have a look at it for you. And good thing, cause it looks like it could be a big one."

"It is big," Carmel said with gritted teeth. If Phonse'd done his duty when his uncle had originally requested, she wouldn't have woken up soaked the other day.

He climbed jauntily down the rickety old ladder he'd propped up against the back, and pushed past her to head into the house and then up the stairs.

"Just got to check out the extent of the damage," he said over his back as he disappeared into the recesses of her bedroom. "Oh, wow. Wow," she heard his muffled voice.

She flinched, remembering how she'd torn off her clothes and strewn them any which way the previous night, more worried about a murderer in the cove than being unnaturally tidy. Hey, it had been a while since any other person had been her bedroom, so putting away her clothes each night had fallen off the priority list.

"You should, like, maybe do some laundry," he said as he appeared in the kitchen again.

Okay, so perhaps there was a couple of days' worth of clothes lying around. "I don't have my mother here to take care of that," she said in an icy voice, but only half-heartedly as she was aware that her snide remark was probably sailing over the head of its intended mark. Sadly, she was right.

"It sure is a mess up there," he agreed. "And that leak—hoo! You must have gotten soaked with that rain the other night. I'll put a patch on that now, won't be a second."

Darrow's warning about hiring a reliable contractor sounded in her mind, but then a vision of her daydream drifted right in front of that. The man from the cove was only trying to help, after all. What was the harm?

Besides, she counter-argued with herself, since she'd found out about his shenanigans with Roxanne, Carmel wasn't going to put up with any nonsense from him. She'd make sure he did a good job, for after all, he owed it to his Uncle Frank.

Phonse poked his head around the back door. "Grab me a beer from the fridge, would you?" he said before going back out. "I saw some in there earlier."

She found herself going to the fridge, mystified as to why he'd been poking around in her kitchen, but soon saw that another slice had been cut from the pie, and the plastic wrap had not been replaced. *The nerve of him*, she thought indignantly. But she took a beer for him anyway, as he probably would appreciate it after fixing the roof for her in this heat. She took it outside, where she could hear his hammer going again, this time replacing the shingles with a small piece of plywood.

"Come on up and join me," he said extending his hand down the ladder. He grabbed the beer from her and left her to struggle her own way up the ladder.

Phonse looked askance at the bottle in his hand. "Can't wait for the strike to be over," he said. "This foreign crap is god-awful."

"I happen to like it," Carmel growled at him as she swung her leg over onto the roof.

He tentatively took a swallow, distaste showing on his face, then settled back against the crumbly-looking chimney and gave a deep sigh. "What a view."

Carmel scrambled off the ladder and on to the part of the roof that was flatter. The plywood gleamed brightly in the sun.

"Is that it?" she asked, noting that he had tucked his hammer back into his tool belt.

"That'll hold it for now," he said. "Until I get some replacement shingles up here."

Was that what he told his uncle? she wondered. How long had Frank Ryan been waiting for the new shingles?

"How's the captain doing?" he asked, leaning back against the crumbling chimney.

"What captain is that?" she asked, irritated at his attempt to change the subject. She didn't know any captains. She looked back at the pathetic patch job Phonse had left.

"Captain Jeremiah, my ancestor," he told her. "The pirate who built this house. Don't tell me you haven't met him yet?"

"He's dead and long gone," she replied. "How long is it going to take you to get this roof fixed?"

Phonse let out a low chuckle. "You don't believe in ghosts, then," he said. "Yet." He laughed again. "Have you noticed the smell?"

"The only smell in that house is the drains," she said.

Phonse smiled and shook his head, looking out towards the ocean.

"Oh, oh, look out there!" He sat up a little and beckoned her. "No, come closer; you gotta see what I mean."

Feeling uncomfortably close to him under the hot sun, she looked where his finger pointed. There was a large something dancing just under the waves.

"What is it?" she said.

"A pair of beluga whales," he replied, still holding her shoulder tightly. They watched as the small whales jumped and frolicked, till they were drawn away again by the movement of the fish they were hunting. Phonse drank his beer and looked the picture of happiness.

As for Carmel, she was feeling uncomfortably warm sitting in the sun under his embrace. She told herself it was the sun getting to her, and tried to pull herself away. He felt the tug, and turned to look. A small smile played on his lips as he pulled her closer, ever closer, watching the flush rise in her face. She felt the melting inside, but struggled against it. Pulling herself away just as he let go his hold, she almost rolled off the roof.

"Whoa, hold on there!" he cried, reaching out for her in the nick of time. He helped her steady herself then brought out a package from his jeans pocket. With a practiced flick, he rolled a cigarette and lit it in what seemed a single movement. He looked at her speculatively, then offered it to her.

"No," she said, pushing his hand away. Feeling quite outraged by this point, she burst out "What are you doing?" Of course, she was referring to the almost kiss, the small tug-of-war game he was playing.

"Just a smoke," he said. "What could be better in life? Hot sun, cold beer, great view..." She could feel his eyes sliding over to her.

Perhaps he hadn't meant anything by it, she thought, now feeling more confused. No, he hadn't been leaning in to kiss her, *don't be ridiculous,* she told herself. Hell, he'd just spent the night with Roxanne. Not to mention her strong suspicion that he was a Peter Pan man, one of those guys who simply would never grow up. *At our age,* she told herself firmly, *we've given up the bed hopping. Who has the time or energy for it? He doesn't think more of me than... than Bridget!* This thought helped her to relax and enjoy the moment. He was right, it was perfect up here from the seagull's view of the cove, the slight wind cooling from the ocean. She looked around and noticed fuzzy moss growing on the shingles. She hoped that wasn't too bad a thing.

"How about that trip to Bell Island tomorrow?" he asked her, eyes closed as he fully enjoyed his buzz. "I can take you to a little beach that you can only get to by boat. It's got some interesting things there you won't see anywhere else."

"How about the roof?" she asked, still eyeing the moss.

"It's not going anywhere," he said. "Besides, it's going to be a bit of job. The summer's too short, let's enjoy it while we can."

She thought a moment. She'd promised a series of short articles on the 'island's islands,' and this could be field research. As with all her work, she wanted to show unique aspects that were off the usual tourist track. This could work out. She just hoped Roxanne would understand that she wasn't making a move on him.

"I could really go for a trip on the water," she replied. He opened an eye in surprise and coughed a little on the swig of beer in his mouth.

"Excellent," he said when he recovered. "You pack us a picnic lunch, and bring some of this beer, if that's all you got. I've got a cooler," he added graciously.

"You're on," she said, accepting his terms. It would be cheaper than hiring a boat to take her out around there, wouldn't it? Even if she took her own car out on the ferry, she needed someone with local knowledge to introduce her to the unique and unknown gems. And he was pleasant enough company, once you got past the good looks, bronzed body and total lack of responsibility.

"Now," she said, looking all around her and for the first time realizing how far away the ground was. "How do we get off this roof?"

Back at her desk yet again, she tried to get her mind back on the murder spreadsheet, but it refused to stick there. The day was cooling off, and she felt the need for action, to busy her body while her mind was left free to chase its thoughts.

I could go look for some more blueberries, she thought, wondering at the same time where Bridget was. The cottage across the road looked to be shut up tight. Perhaps Bridget was off selling her pottery. She had to make a living somehow, and she didn't appear to sell from her house.

Carmel set out through the woods with buckets in hand, looking for the path they'd taken a few days ago, but with no success. She gave up after a while, thinking that if she just aimed to go uphill, she couldn't lose. At last, she re-found the stone ledge where they'd sat overlooking the water and climbed up further to the blueberry barrens.

Looking down, she realized she could see right into Melba's back yard. There were no signs of life there, although the back door was wide open so she must be around somewhere close. This sparked an idea. Darrow had asked for her help when he pointed out that as an outsider living in this close-knit community, she was in a unique position to help him gain insight into his inquiries. This was a license to snoop, surely. Although she was a person who'd always kept very much to herself, as a writer she was naturally nosey, and now could use her skills to help get to the bottom of this horrendous crime.

What information exactly was she to be looking for? she wondered as she picked the berries. The police would have interviewed any likely suspect, asked what they were doing at the time of the murder, and if they held a grudge against Peters (everybody here seemed to). She fervently wished she could have access to what they'd discovered in their interviews, but she knew Darrow would not be forthcoming. She had to ask herself, *what could she find out that the police with all their resources couldn't?*

And then it dawned on her. The inhabitants of the cove, with their shared history and family ties, would no doubt band together in the face of the law, protecting each other. Smuggling, piracy and other lawless activities were part of their shared heritage, and perhaps it was no coincidence that St. Jude Without had remained, as Darrow aptly put it, 'under the radar.' She was already infiltrated within the community, and she could discover the story behind the one that had been presented to the police. If the cove was hiding something, she vowed she'd find it out, if just for her own satisfaction.

It didn't take long to fill the white buckets, and she headed back down the mountain towards Melba's cottage. The tiny paths she could find were not straightforward, of course—just trails made by rabbits or moose, petering out just when she thought she'd found a way. But it wasn't long before Hank the cat found her, and by following him through the bushes and over the rocks, she soon found herself overlooking Melba's back door.

The garden was a perfect cottage garden in full bloom, even this late in the short growing season. Old fashioned white roses bloomed on a bush next to the last of the mallow and daisies, while the late summer phlox perfumed the air pink. Tall monkshood and foxglove towered at the back, their flowers fading as they turned to seed. An ancient wooden folding chair stood next to a small iron table by the back door, showing where Melba enjoyed the passing of an afternoon.

She followed the path down the small hillock, only noticing when she'd descended that she had, in fact, been on top of a root cellar. This man-made structure resembled a hobbit house with one dry stone wall emerging from the very land itself and its roof long since sodded over with tall late summer grass. The stout wooden door, the paint weathered off, shone silver in the late light of day. A thick branch propped the door firmly closed.

"Hello?" she called out into the empty clearing. Hank chirped as well. She'd never get used to such a small sound coming from that large cat. Had anyone told him he was no longer a kitten?

"Melba," she said as the old woman materialized just inside the open door. "Hi, I've brought you some blueberries."

Melba blinked at the buckets, then took both in her hands. Carmel hesitated at this, as she'd only intended to give her one bucket's worth and keep the other for freezing, but she let it go. All for a good cause.

"Well, bless you, girl," she said, although Carmel would never see forty again. "And I was just thinking it was time to haul my old bones up the hill to go berry picking. You must have read my mind. Come in, dear, come in and join me for a cup of tea."

The Irish and British heritage showed in this cove, as all over the island, when tea was offered as a matter of course for all occasions. This time it was served in a proper pot, with matching cups and saucers of the most delicate china, hand-painted with violets amid greenery. Sweet rectangular cakes and cookies were set out on a matching plate, the kind of comforting home baking available at every church sale.

"This is a beautiful china set," Carmel observed as she took one of the sweets offered. Hank was settling uncomfortably into her lap, turning and twisting, looking for the perfect angle upon which to rest his twenty pound mass.

"Twas my grandmother's wedding set," Melba said. "Came over from Ireland with her, and I've kept it good all these years. The only plate broken was the time young Phonse got greedy and tried to snatch a whole handful of bars before Sid could get at them. What a pair of rascals they was, growing up."

Carmel was offered neither milk nor sugar to go with her tea, and she was thinking the tea looked rather pale and anemic compared to the usual strong brew served. The old woman must have noticed the look of perturbation on her face as she gazed into the cup.

"It's mallow tea," she told the younger woman. "Good for whatever ails you. I always take a cup of mallow in the morning and at this hour." She waved her hand around at the garden. "God gives us everything we need in nature. No need for doctors when you've got a garden."

As they chatted, Carmel surreptitiously looked around the ancient kitchen. The pots and pans hanging on the walls were battered and heavy iron, showing evidence of good use over many years. A huge fireplace took up all of one wall, showing the true age of the building to be perhaps two hundred years old. Rafters were hung with drying herbs like oregano and rosemary, and other flora that Carmel couldn't identify. And all around the ledges were candles—mostly white, but some black—all of them half burnt down. The whole room resembled a witch's cottage from a fairy-tale. In the pantry by the back door, she could see that Melba kept her gardening items on the counter, the long sharp secateurs and ancient cracked leather gardening gloves. *Where would she keep her fish knives?* Carmel wondered.

The old woman had a sharp memory, and a fine turn of wit. In fact, reigning over her kitchen, she was the picture of sanity and Carmel began to doubt her impressions of the other day. Could she have misinterpreted the old woman's words? Melba knew a story about everyone in the cove—if Carmel could choose the subject carefully, the old woman might tell her something valuable about what had led up to the murder.

When she carefully steered the conversation to the present century, of course, the subject of the murder arose.

"All's well that ends well," Melba said on the subject, with a satisfied expression on her face.

Carmel, taken aback, didn't know how to reply.

"Oh, I've shocked you, haven't I, dear?" said the old lady, a gentle smile on her face. "He really was a bad one, you know, that Eric Peters, and his brother isn't much better. Yes, Eric deserved everything he got."

"Did you hear anything that night?" Carmel asked. "I mean, it took place right at the bottom of your laneway."

"Oh, I'll not tell what I heard," the old lady said, her smile turning secretive. "And I certainly didn't tell that policeman, lovely as he was. I don't sleep as soundly as I used to. No one will know what I saw that night."

She leaned over the table and whispered, "He should have known better than to upset the fairies, you know."

Oh well, so much for sanity, Carmel thought wearily. "I don't think it was magical beings that did the murder," she said. "His throat was cut with a fish gutting knife."

A sound at the back door caused them both to look up. Bridget was standing there, hands on hips, a dark glare on her face. Roxanne stood just behind her, her eyes on Melba.

"Aunt Melba, you stop that nonsense, now," Bridget said. "Carmel, don't listen to her foolishness."

"Not foolishness, young Bridget," the old woman replied. "I'm sure there's some around here that wouldn't like me to tell what I know."

Bridget remained in the doorway, standing stock still, her face pale and her brow set.

"Don't you care at all?" she cried at the old woman. "Can you not just leave it alone?" Then she turned and ran out of the porch, out of the yard and down the lane.

Carmel, mystified at what had just passed between the two, took one look at the old lady cackling with a nasty glee, and followed to help her friend. Roxanne hesitated, then nodded to Melba and quickly caught up with Carmel.

Chapter 7

That scene had been plenty weird. Bridget had refused to talk with either Carmel or Roxanne. Instead, she'd locked herself in her house. Why was Bridget so upset at Melba's claim to know who the murderer was? Once she really turned herself to answering that question, Carmel's mind reeled because there were so many possibilities—none of which led to the same conclusion, and none of which she liked. One, Bridget was the murderer Melba saw, and naturally Bridget didn't want the old woman spreading the word. No, that couldn't possibly have worked—Bridget might have had time to run down to the bridge, but how likely was it? It could only have happened if Bridget had pre-arranged to meet Peters, otherwise she wouldn't have known he was down there waiting to be attacked. On the other hand, maybe Bridget went down that way to check on Melba with the storm coming, noticed Peters standing around and slit his throat with a cut-throat she just happened to have in the voluminous pocket of her hippie cotton dress along with her tankard and crystal goblet? Very unlikely.

Get back to the list. Two, Melba was the murderer. Bridget knew this and was trying to protect her. Or, along the same lines, both of them knew the identity of the person from the cove who *was* Peters' killer, and Bridget wanted to protect the person and didn't want Melba telling.

Or three, an option which had nothing whatsoever to do with the murder. Bridget knew Melba was slightly senile and didn't want the evidence of that spread around. Didn't both Bridget and Phonse insist that they looked after their own in the Cove? If Community Services found out about Melba, an old woman living alone in the woods in her senility, they'd want to remove her to a nice safe nursing home in the city, a world away from her cottage in the cove. Carmel didn't know Melba very well, but well enough to know the old woman would be miserable in that situation. She was happy enough living with her fairies and cat for company.

Carmel had to take her mind away from all this— these divergent lines of thought weren't getting her anywhere. Besides, she had to catch the news, just to watch how the nasty Vee Ryan had comported herself in front of the camera. Gerald Smythe and his crew had been down at the little bungalow for a good two hours.

"More on the mysterious murder of Eric Peters," she caught Smythe's smooth voice-over to yesterday's footage of the police cars and the bright yellow tape fluttering off the bridge.

The cameras opened on Gerald Smythe in front of the weathered church sign. Carmel realized this old sign was the only indicator of place name in the community. Against the gray cliff face to his right, Smythe's lurid pink shirt was the only bright spot to be seen.

"The village of St. Jude Without," he said portentously. "But the question on everyone's mind is, what is it exactly that St. Jude is without? A good coffee bar? Uhh." He paused for his silent laugh track again, then graced his audience with his naughty little boy grin. Oops, he'd done it yet again.

"Seriously, now," he said, his close-set features screwing up to take his own advice. "The place where Eric Peters was murdered is one strange little cove." He leaned in as the camera panned closer.

"Incest and inbreeding?" he asked, raising his eyebrows in a mockery of concern. "Drugs?" The camera backed away to include the motorcycles in its frame.

"Probably," he confided. "Prostitution?"

A shot of the teenagers aping for Smythe flashed on the screen. Their tank tops had dropped a little to reveal more lacy bras, while the skirts were hitched up even higher. One of them must have found a black eyeliner, for now all their eyes were ringed in kohl. There would be hell to pay in the cove that evening after the news was over.

"Who knows what evil lurks here?" He looked hard into the camera lens. "Tonight, I have an insider's view of the cove. An interview with Mrs. Ryan who claims that everyone in this village is related, and some other dark secrets of the cove. Definitely a small gene pool, if you get my drift." He winked into the camera before the screen cut to the inside of what must be Vee's house.

It was a museum of kitsch, dedicated to years of bad taste and a reluctance to let go of the past. Like most kitchens in the Cove, the popular renovation movement of granite counters and stainless steel appliances had completely passed it by, and the last re-fit might have been sometime in the late sixties. The avocado fridge stood wheezing alone next to the red Formica-topped table with its chrome chairs upholstered in the original vinyl. Hand-carved gingerbread decorated the top of the window with its lace curtains shielding the family's privacy from the prying eyes of sea-going vessels. The camera panned all around the small kitchen, slowly focusing on the china kittens, burnt-wood plaques and plastic flowers, before reaching Gerald's astounded face as he rolled his eyes and shrugged in mock horror. A smile became fixed to his face as Vee bustled into view setting down a tray with the formal teapot, cups and saucers she brought out for company.

"The cameras aren't rolling yet, are they?" she asked as she made adjustments to her bra and skirt.

"Why, no," he told her, smirking and winking into the lens behind her back.

The televised interview must have been created with bits and pieces of the whole, with Gerald's voice over asking the questions, continuing along the nasty course he'd started with. Watching it, Carmel couldn't help wondering if Vee had imbibed a little whiskey with her tea over the course of the afternoon, so uninhibited did she appear. Of course, with clever editing, any impression could be given.

"Yes, the fairies in the wood," Vee was nodding to the reporter. "Some says it's true." There was a pause as the picture jumped to a slight change of angle, and her voice continued in a different tone. "And I believe it!"

Carmel realized Smythe was paying back the cove for snubbing him, by making the community he now despised appear to be ridiculous—its population a comedic cast of Shakespearean proportions. That he despised them all was evident. To finish off this terrible abuse of editing masquerading as an interview, Smythe was again shown standing by the church.

"And so, through this painstaking investigative journalism, I've discovered incest, drugs, even fairies now in the equation," he told the camera, his face a mask of disbelief. "What is happening in this strange, strange cove they call St. Jude Without?" The screen flashed through shots of the community and its residents, including Clyde cursing and shaking his fist, a close-up of Sid and his friends roaring off so it looked like a full gang of bikers and lastly, and what really stung, a shot of herself and Bridget peering through a window, convulsed with glee like village idiots.

All the media was having a high time of it. Even the local call-in radio show in the city poked its fun the next morning while she ate breakfast.

"So callers," the announcer said, "the question of the day is—'Who Killed Eric Peters?' The police certainly aren't getting anywhere with this, so we want you to call in. Maybe you can solve the mystery for us!

"John G, you're on the line. Any ideas? Another vote for the bikers? Alright, our tally shows…"

She had to turn it off. This was not just a circus, but a full-fledged carnival.

To clear her head, she decided to walk back out to Portugal Cove and that lovely little coffee shop. Again, the news crews weren't out this early in the morning. As she was walking in the quiet morning, she got to thinking again of the list she'd started the previous day. The mayor in Portugal Cove, she realized, could have easily walked to and from the cove without using a vehicle, and would have been able to bypass the camera at the ferry terminal. She was sure that this angle hadn't come up for Inspector Darrow. The policeman had been certain the murderer was someone in the cove itself, and so was concentrating his efforts there. Yeah, it was a long shot—a murdering mayor intent on expanding his fiefdom, but she'd read lots of book which had stranger plots. She wondered how she could present herself to him in order to ask the right questions.

Carmel needn't have worried about searching out the mayor for he was holding court again at the coffee shop over a hearty and full breakfast. After she'd introduced herself and mentioned she was living in St. Jude Without, he grabbed the conversation and took it exactly where she wanted it to go.

"I'm glad to see outsiders moving in there finally," he said. "The place needs new blood—full of hillbillies and hippies who can't be bothered to drag themselves into the twenty-first century. That's one thing Smythe got right last night."

The short, round man quickly got on his figurative soapbox, explaining again the desperate need for amalgamation which was a major bee in his bonnet. She prodded him back to the development scheme and Eric Peters.

"Why wouldn't Peters have pushed to join the larger community?" she asked. "After all, he would want access to water and sewers, roads, garbage pickup…?"

The mayor, whose name, by the way, was Thomas Ryan and who claimed not to be related to the 'inbred' Ryans of the next cove over, slammed his fist on the table so hard his round cheeks wobbled and his fork fell off the plate.

"Peters didn't give a damn about any community," he said. "He most certainly didn't want the cove to join a larger town, because he didn't want to pay any taxes or have inspectors breathing down his neck during the building phase. You look at the houses he built in the center of the city two years ago. The owners are already complaining that the siding is coming off their houses and the windows are leaking. The only reason he'd gotten away with it for all those years," the little man said passionately across the table, "The only reason he'd gotten away with his cheap-jack housing builds was because of his brother and political connections."

Carmel already knew how awful Peters had been, even in her short contact with the man, so there was no need to let Thomas Ryan rehash this ground. "Did I overhear you saying yesterday that the mountain could be a Heritage site?" she asked him.

Mayor Ryan again went over his theory on the last of the Beothuks on the Avalon for her benefit.

"I've seen archeological evidence on Farrell's land, years ago, that was. If I could just get a team over there, we could have it proclaimed a Heritage site, build a museum and have a destination for tourists. So close to the city, it would be huge," he insisted. "The road would be paved and that sorry little cove could be opened up to the world, whether they liked it or not."

She winced as spit hit her forehead above her left eye and tried not to dab it away immediately. She sincerely hoped it wasn't a piece of egg.

"So the end of the proposed development is a good thing for you?" she asked.

The man took a sip of coffee and looked at her speculatively.

"Not just the end of the development, but how it ended," he said, his voice much lowered now.

He nodded as if in answer to an unspoken question and tapped the side of his nose.

"We all know who did Peters in," he said. "And when the police find the evidence they need, he'll have to sell that farm of his to pay his defense lawyer."

"You mean…"

"Oh, yes, my dear," he replied. "Oh, yes. It's not the first dark deed the man has done, but this time he'll be caught. When Farrell's out of the way, my museum— the tribute to the Beothuk—will become a reality."

The small boat bobbed over the Tickle and around the head of Bell Island. The sun glanced off the waves dancing in the cool breeze, and Carmel shivered slightly, drawing her sweater closer. Phonse hadn't been kidding when he'd advised her to dress warm for the short trip on the water, even on this warm afternoon.

Of course, she had an ulterior motive in joining him on this trip, not just for research on her article. She wanted to pick his brains a little to see what she could uncover. She was beginning to think she had a knack for this investigation business.

He pointed ahead of them to the single tall stack of solid rock rising from the water, separated from the other cliffs by a narrow rush of water.

"That there is called the clapper. You know, because it's at the end of Bell Island?" he said, ensuring she got the point. "And there's a lighthouse on top of the main cliff. You can't see it from below, of course."

Carmel gazed up and up at the solid wall of rock rising before her. She felt quite dizzy. Gulls and other seabirds circled and whirled and endlessly cried, hundreds of them it seemed.

"You'll want to keep your mouth closed," Phonse warned as a white missile splatted on the deck. She closed it quickly and drew up the hood of her sweater to protect her hair.

He drew the boat into a tiny cove of rocky pebbles. Tall cliffs surrounded the small grassy knoll above the beach, with not even a goat path leading down to the shore. He cut the motor and dropped anchor. Leaping out in his high rubber boots, he told her to take off her Converse slip-ons and help pull the boat up on the shingle a little. The water was freezing, even now at the end of this hot summer, and her feet were quickly numb. She hopped up to the shore as soon as she could.

A quick cup of coffee from the thermos helped warm her up again. In fact, out of the open breezy sea air, it quickly became sweltering in the tiny sheltered cove. They wandered around the small beach for a while. Along the tide's edge were special rocks of all colours and stripes, purple and red and green with blue running through them, all worn by the constant action of water and rock against rock. Impressed as she was by their vivid hues while wet, she knew once they dried they would lose their magic. She was disappointed that she found little in this small area that was very remarkable, at least not enough to base an article on as Phonse had promised.

They companionably sat in the long grass, their legs dangling over the hummock leading to the beach, listening to the susurration of the pebbles being washed by the waves, the whispering sound having a lulling effect. The cruise in the open salt air had whetted her appetite so she stirred herself to dig around inside of the knapsack for the food and beer. As they ate, they talked the loose talk of friends on a late summer afternoon. He lit up the usual hand-made cigarette, but again she declined, bringing out her own cigarette pack and allowing him to offer her a light.

"How do I describe this in words," she asked, leaning back on to the grass, her eyes closed. "I thought I could do research for my article this afternoon, find something interesting I can sell to the armchair tourists. Instead, I've found heaven—how can I describe that?"

She heard the grass rustle beneath him as he shifted his weight, then sensed him move over her, blocking out the sun's brightness on her eyelids. Feeling the nearing warmth of his body as he drew close, she lazily thought how perfect it could all be if only it wasn't this man. Or if she still had a crush on him, which she certainly didn't. His lips met hers, his breath hot on her face and she felt her body surrendering down. Her mind refused to let that happen.

Carmel struggled up, pushing him back with her arm.

"No," she said, breathlessly sitting up, shaking her head.

"What?" He looked flabbergasted and not a little put out. "What's wrong?"

It was her turn to look surprised.

"What do you mean what's wrong?" she asked, amazed that he had the nerve to come on to her, and the audacity to ask what was wrong with this picture. "What do you *think* is wrong?"

He stared at her, his bright blue eyes uncomprehending.

"Did I say I wanted to do this?" she said. "You think I came over here with you just to get laid on a beach?"

"Well, why else would you come?" he asked crossly.

She opened her mouth to reply, but caught herself at the last moment, realizing she couldn't tell him she was investigating which of his close relatives was a murderer.

He stood up and began to rant in his sexual disappointment.

"You go on a boat with a guy to an isolated cove to have sex, don't you?" he said. "Everyone knows that. I mean, come on, 'going to Bell Island' is a cliché for god's sake. Why the hell else would you come here with me?"

"I can't believe you!" She found herself standing up and fighting back. "You .... slut! You male-slut! After what passed between you and Roxanne the other night, and you're here bitching at me because I won't screw you?"

At this point, she would normally have stormed from the room, but there was nowhere else to go.

His eyes lit up in understanding.

"Oh, that." He laughed, his frustration put behind him. *He actually laughed*, she thought, *How could he?*

"Nah, nah. That was nothing," he said, waving his hand deprecatingly and shaking his head. "She... oh that girl, I tell you."

"Would Roxanne also say it was nothing?" she asked icily. "You shared her bed for a night, and it was nothing?"

Carmel was so glad she hadn't given in to his charms. The man was turning out to be a total bastard.

"Yes, she would." He laughed even harder. "You don't really think me and Roxanne..."

What was this? They didn't....? Her heart gave a sudden swoop of joy, totally bypassing the other issue and her common sense.

"She certainly gave that impression," Carmel replied, hesitating, then pulled herself together for this was a dilemma she couldn't ignore. "And hey, that's what she told the police. Didn't she tell them you were with her all night after the bar, which meant you couldn't have done in Peters?"

"She only said that to help me out, though," he said, as if that made it alright, his guileless blue eyes crinkling in the sun. "I'd dropped into her place 'cause she'd left a note for me to turn her water back on. But just one minute, I swear. She didn't even offer me a drink."

His whole face smiled innocently at her, delighted to have cleared up that misunderstanding. His arms reached out to her to recapture the moment. "She didn't lie," he insisted. "She never said I was there all night, now, did she?"

Carmel stared, for the second time that afternoon almost speechless. Would he never cease to amaze?

"This means you have no alibi for the night Peters was murdered?" she said quietly.

"No, I don't," he said, the smile slowly falling from his face. "But that's okay, because I didn't do it." He looked at her earnestly.

"You lied to the police," she said, pressing the point.

"No," he said firmly, then sighed. "Roxanne misled the police, if you insist on putting it like that. They didn't ask me about it; they assumed I had an alibi."

"Do you not see how wrong that is?" she exploded finally, her disappointment all the sharper now.

"But I didn't do it," he said, spelling it out for her yet again. The temperature on the tiny beach dropped several degrees as the sun left his eyes, clouds rising above their heads.

She could not speak to him any longer after that, caught in this dilemma. This man for whom she'd felt an instant attraction (and that didn't happen often these days) turns out not to be sleeping with another woman, but instead was the main suspect in a murder investigation and was, in essence, lying to the police. And he saw nothing wrong with that.

What to do? Carmel fully believed that he hadn't cut Peters throat like a thief in the night. She felt sure if Phonse ever killed a man, it would be in an outright passionate (albeit perhaps drunken) one-on-one fight. And, despite the present quandary, Phonse was not a dishonest man. Not really. She could feel that in her very bones.

And she knew if she let him keep talking, she just might see the sense in his argument. The police would like to pin it on him, given his record for bar room fights and suspected smuggling activities. It would make their problem of solving the murder go away, and a quick wrap-up always looked good on the books. The question was did her loyalty lie with the side of right or with this gorgeous innocent scoff-law?

They rode the short distance over the tickle to the cove in silence. The sun had now fully disappeared and the wind on the water came straight from the Arctic, cutting like a knife through the loose knit of her sweater. He brought the boat in and tied it at the wharf, and helped her out of the boat without another word passing between them.

There was no way Carmel was going to take the short cut over the gorge to the road past where she'd found Peters' body splayed out over the rock. As she passed Phonse's house, her head held high, she could see out of the corner of her eye his mother pinning up his tighty-white underwear on the clothesline, gossiping over the fence with Ida.

"Bell Island, eh?" she heard the women snigger. "That was a quick one."

"Really? Bell Island?" Bridget looked at her. She had just let herself in the back door, thumping her way into Carmel's kitchen to announce her presence.

"Nice to see you too, Bridget." Carmel looked up from her laptop, a mug halfway to her mouth. She hoped the sarcasm was evident. "Why don't you come on in?"

"I am in," Bridget replied humourlessly and sat opposite. The pink of her long dress clashed awfully with her hair, sallowing her complexion. "I just can't believe you, of all people...."

Carmel was beginning to feel more and more as Alice had after her tumble into the rabbit-hole.

"Me?" she asked. "What have I done?" She felt justifiably outraged. After all, Carmel was not the one colluding in a lie to the police.

"It's just tacky, that's all. I thought better of you than that."

"It was a boat trip, nothing more. I didn't go out to... you know."

"Yeah but, did you...?"

"Lord no!"

"Then why go out there at all? Didn't you think people would talk? The whole cove saw you guys heading out there. And at your age."

"How was I supposed to know the courting traditions of St. Jude Without?" she replied, just a little stung by the reference to age. "I wanted to see Bell Island, he offered to take me out there. End of story."

"And Phonse of all people," Bridget continued. "That's just... gross."

"He's a very attractive man, even at 'his age.'" Carmel didn't know why she was defending him. "But I didn't go out there for ... that."

The two sat in silence for a moment.

"Have you ever gone..." Carmel asked.

"Oh yeah," replied Bridget quickly. She looked up and flashed a grin. The storm had passed. "Not with my cousin though."

Carmel wondered if there was anyone in the cove who wasn't related to Bridget, but decided to drop that line of thought. She looked at the younger woman across the table who was helping herself to the contents of the teapot, still hot under the knitted cosy. She couldn't be a murderer, surely? Carmel found it difficult to even think of Bridget as harbouring a killer, but she'd seen first hand the strength of the woman's loyalty. What lengths would she go to protect the people and the home she loved? She really liked Bridget, and appreciated her quick wit. Carmel needed someone to talk over her suspicions with, but she knew that person just couldn't be Bridget. She had to talk with Darrow again.

Chapter 8

The opportunity arose just that evening. Another lovely end of day, with another perfect sunset over the bay, Carmel poured herself a glass of white wine (a real wine glass this time, for she'd managed to unpack most of her kitchen) and settled on the veranda. Inspector Darrow's grey sedan drove up right at that moment, his timing impeccable.

"Still on duty?" she called down as he closed the car door behind him.

"This job is never over," he joked, climbing the steps. The sleeves of his pale blue shirt were rolled up in homage to the lingering summer weather, but the tie remained firmly ensconced around his neck.

He eased himself into the second plastic Adirondack chair.

"Haven't seen much police presence in the cove today," she said.

He shook his head.

"No, not much headway here," he said. "The George Street riots have been taking up our time. Even after the storm cleared the air and turned the weather around the other night, it didn't dampen the roar. The RNC want to close down the entire street, but the government won't let us, what with the election coming this fall. They don't want to be accused of fascism. Yet the government is still screaming at us to finish this case, naturally. You know where their priorities lie."

Carmel bit her lip. She knew she had to tell him about how Roxanne had misled the police. She also knew what would happen to Phonse if she did, for Bridget was right. She trusted Darrow to do the right thing, but his higher-ups might be more politically motivated. Phonse would be taken into custody and the murder pinned on him without too much ceremony or further ado, the case neatly tied up and the premier satisfied that justice was done for his name.

Even if Phonse was innocent, which she felt deep down inside he was. But it didn't look good.

She took a deep breath and told him what she'd learned. He listened quietly.

"This is a pretty serious allegation," he said.

Carmel nodded miserably.

He sighed and pinched the bridge of his nose. "So as far as you know, the man has lied to the police as to his whereabouts that night," he ascertained, his deep Scottish burr showing his tiredness. Carmel nodded, and hesitated. There was something else at the back of her mind, something about Phonse's boat. She desperately searched her mind, but couldn't get a grasp on it.

"You're the policeman, then?" A large form had materialized at the gate, the voice a screechful of unpleasantry.

"It's about my Phonse," the woman continued, forcing back the gate and heavily stomping her way up the wooden steps. "I'm here to tell you that that slut told you a pack of lies."

Having been labeled so by the woman previously, Carmel wondered what the woman had on her mind. Remembering her ill treatment at Mrs. Ryan's hands the day she'd found the body, she felt her face growing hot.

"I'm not the liar around here," she defended herself hotly.

"Not you slut, the other slut," Mrs. Ryan dismissed her. "The smart one."

She'd reached the top stair by now, her bulk blocking the view. Slightly breathless from the climb, she continued.

"She told you my Phonse spent the night with her," she said. "Well, that's not true. He's not that kind of boy."

That the 'boy' was over forty-five years of age was not an apparent irony to the woman.

"I waits up for him every night," she said, "and he came in before ten o'clock, just like he always does, so as not to worry his poor mother. He always warns me if he's going to be late."

She nodded emphatically.

"I likes to go to bed knowing he's safe and sound," she added with a martyred air. "If you'd bothered to ask me, I would have told you the truth long before."

"Tell me, Mrs. Ryan," Inspector Darrow said slowly, "did he come in before the rain started, or after?"

"It was just about to start," she replied. "He even said to me, 'Mudder,' he said, 'Mudder, I think I got in just in time. The winds getting up and it's going to pour out there.' I seen him making his way back from that hussy's house. He was just there a minute or two. Sleeping over with her, indeed."

Darrow nodded. "And can you vouch that he stayed home all night?"

Mrs. Ryan looked suitably shocked. "Course he did," she said. "Where else would he be going at that hour of night? I took meself off to bed, and he shut up the house as he always does. I could hear him snoring away before I got to sleep myself, louder than the rain even."

"An officer will be by to take a statement tomorrow morning, Mrs. Ryan," the Inspector said. "But may I ask you, what was he wearing when he came back in?"

"Well, his white t-shirt, like he always wears," she replied. "I remember saying and it was a good thing he got in when he did, otherwise he might catch a cold, just wearing that at night."

That this righteous lady spoke the truth as she knew it, there was no doubt. Having established her son's alibi and straightened the policeman out, she turned and heavily clomped off down the steps and down the lane towards her home.

"That changes things," the Inspector said, after a pause. "Phonse came in before the rain started. His white t-shirt would have had blood splattered all over it if he'd been the one to slit Peters' throat."

"If she's telling the truth," Carmel added with doubt in her voice. Mrs. Ryan did everything for her grown son, and would probably lie to save him. But the conviction in the woman's voice rang true.

Darrow left not too long after, for his work wasn't yet finished for the day. It was only after he'd gone that Carmel remembered that she still hadn't told him what Melba had said, that the old woman had claimed to know who the murderer was. Still, she comforted herself, time enough for that later. And Melba was not necessarily a reliable witness, confusing fairy stories with reality as she did. She thought about the old woman's words again and shook her head. No, she wouldn't call him back over this, for likely as not it would just be a red herring, causing unnecessary work for the police, and they had enough untruths to deal with. She had a sneaking suspicion that Melba had originally told the truth, and had made this up for attention.

Her thoughts wandered on to Roxanne. The Englishwoman appeared to be so solid and hale, like a grown-up girl scout really. Educated, well-travelled— Carmel would have said she was practical and sensible. But what had led her to mislead the investigation as she had? Phonse didn't spend the night with her, but she'd been trying to protect him.

Although she appeared to be hewn of solid rock, the woman was a softie inside. And a romantic, Carmel realized, remembering how aflutter she'd been the first time they'd met, when Roxanne's eyes lit up at the mention of Phonse. A woman could easily develop a crush on the gorgeousness which was that fisherman, as Carmel knew to her own dismay, and her heart warmed towards the humanity of the other woman, that seemingly crusty shell which covered a romantic heart, just like her own. A woman alone, also like herself.

"I'm going to go clear the air," she decided on the spur of the moment. "She's probably embarrassed now, and I don't want ill-feeling between us. I think we could be pretty good friends."

With that, she set off on the gravelled dusty road into the sunset, down the point of land at the end of which Roxanne resided. There was no sign of Phonse or (thank God) Vee, though she would have gladly taken the woman on at this point.

Us sluts got to stick together against the bullies of the world, she thought vehemently as she passed the lane to the wharf and surreptitiously stuck out her tongue in the direction of Vee's house. The lace at a window quivered. It could have been the ocean breeze and not the malevolent woman spying on her, but Carmel picked up her pace and hastened on.

When she finally reached the small cottage, she realized she had no idea what she was planning to say to Roxanne. Spurred on by visions of female solidarity in the face of all the uncaring men and their horrible mothers in the world, she had marched down the road like a Crusader to save Jerusalem, but how exactly did one introduce these lofty thoughts into a conversation?

She needn't have worried, for the English woman was delighted to see her and greeted her warmly.

"Have you eaten? I've got a spinach salad with strawberries. Just a light supper, but there's plenty to share," Roxanne said. "Please say yes," she continued as she bustled about to set another place at the table.

Of course. Food. It seemed all she did around here was eat. Really, she'd have to start thinking seriously about exercise.

"About Phonse the other night..." Carmel had to bring it up and get that over with quickly or she wouldn't be able to rest.

Roxanne set the fork carefully in its place and looked up at her, gauging her mood. "Yes."

"He didn't stay with you that night, right?"

Roxanne's shoulders relaxed and she laughed, brushing it aside. "Oh, that," she said. "He *did* come to see me," she continued. "But only for a minute, and then he went right home across the meadow."

"But why lie about it?"

She faced Carmel across the table. "I saw him looking at you, at the bar that night," she said softly, her face reddening. "I could tell I didn't have a chance with him. I didn't want the murder pinned on him, and I wanted you to keep away from him." She turned away. "Pretty stupid thing to do, right?"

Carmel couldn't disagree, but she felt better about it all now. It couldn't have been an easy thing for Roxanne to admit.

"He's all yours, believe me," she told her, and Roxanne shook her head. They laughed together.

As Roxanne served up the salad, Carmel looked around the small cottage. It was a tiny space, its very simplicity a quiet statement of its age. One large room with two smaller ones leading directly off it. The layout was one used perhaps by pioneers everywhere, frontier people who were only glad to have a roof over their heads and who, building the home themselves with materials cut from the woods by their own hands, were ever conscious of their priorities. This home may have been among the first built on the point, back in the time when Farrell's forebears were scourging the land of natives and French, for the style had changed little over the early years of English settlement. The relatively flat, rock-free land surrounding it would have been ideal for the necessary vegetable garden to tide them through a scurvy-free winter. No doubt there would be a root cellar nearby, like the one in Melba's garden, to store the harvest back in the years before refrigerators became common.

There was very little of Roxanne's personality in this rented home, Carmel could see, which made sense as the English woman's work caused her to lead a nomadic lifestyle, travelling through strange lands and living among native peoples. Only a few books in a pile on the coffee table, and a photograph standing in a frame. A knitted throw laid neatly over the sofa and the crocheted pillow covers with lurid synthetic colors had no doubt been made by Vee in years gone by.

"It's a comfortable home," Carmel said as she saw that Roxanne had noticed her inspection of the room.

"Suits me fine," the English woman replied. "I don't need much. Although..." She peered shyly up at Carmel, and hesitated, then smiled. "I really wanted your house," she said as if confessing.

"The view," Carmel said, remembering their first meeting.

The other nodded. "It wasn't available at the time." She picked up her fork to begin her meal, and Carmel followed suit. The salad, like the home they were in, was simple but just what was needed, no more and no less.

"How long are you staying here?" Carmel asked her.

"My lease is just until the middle of September," she said. "Then they've promised it to someone else, another visiting professor. It's been arranged since last year."

Carmel looked up, her fork arrested halfway to her mouth. "But what will you do then? Any plans for travelling again?"

"I hadn't planned on it, I'd really just like to stay in the area for a bit longer."

The two continued with their meal, but Carmel's mind was working. It would be an enormous help financially to rent a room in the house on the hill, especially if she were travelling herself. She dearly wanted to keep the place as a base to which to return, but it would be a stretch to keep paying rent when she might not be there for months at a time. And Roxanne was all right, if a little odd. This could work out nicely, she decided, and made up her mind right then. This was a brilliant idea, and in her impetuous way, she didn't pause to examine it for negative possibilities. What could go wrong?

"How about renting with me?" She casually threw it out, not wanting Roxanne to feel obligated. "Think about it, this could work for both of us."

Roxanne looked up at her, surprised delight dawning in her eyes. "You'd do that? Rent a room to me?" she asked. "That would solve... so much."

"I'd be happy to," Carmel beamed back at her, now smiling largely. "It does get lonely, being single, as you probably know. It would be great to have someone else around, and I'm sure we could manage not to get on each other's nerves."

Carmel lay down her utensil, a grin still plastered on her face. The dressing has been delicious—not too heavy on the oil, but flavorful enough for the light salad. Her new room-mate obviously knew a thing or two about food too—this arrangement was definitely promising.

Roxanne drew in a breath to speak, but her eyes were drawn to Carmel's smile.

"Uh...." she started, as if uncomfortable. She looked away, and pointed to her own mouth. "You have ... in your teeth."

Carmel shut her mouth and covered it with her hand for good measure. "Oh. Spinach. Bathroom?"

"Along there." Roxanne pointed, relieved.

The bathroom was a tiny add-on to the house, hardly big enough for a toilet and a small tub. There were no cosmetics or personal items displayed. She opened the mirrored cabinet over the sink to look for floss or something to pick out the offending vegetation. Carmel always felt a little guilty opening bathroom cabinets, only because it was something she always wanted to do when in someone's home, and the reason behind it was pure nosiness—she loved to peek into people's private lives. She usually forced herself not to do it; however, this time she had to from necessity. Like the house, the small cabinet held little within it of Roxanne's, just two pill bottles with dusty caps, a tub of cream, some ointments and a plastic roll of floss. She grabbed the package of floss, gave a wistful glance at the bottles whose labels were turned inward and did the necessary on her teeth. The cabinet door firmly shut against her nosy parker urges, she returned to the main room where Roxanne had cleared away the remains of the meal.

Roxanne happily chattered about her intended move up the hill later in September. "Do you have linens? Or furnishings? I don't really have much to move, I'm used to living out of my backpack," she said, "as you can probably see."

Carmel was able to grin freely again now that the spaces between her teeth were cleaned. "It's not luxurious, but I'm sure you're used to roughing it."

Her attention turned again to the books on the table. "What are your books?" she asked, knowing just by their presence that they must be special to have a place in the anthropologist's nomadic life. She idly reached over to ruffle through the first, a small thin volume, with an old-fashioned cloth cover. "Sir Arthur Conan Doyle? An old friend. Which one of his is this?"

He'd been an early favorite of hers, right up there with Agatha Christie. She read the title closer. "*The Coming of the Fairies*? I've certainly never heard of this one. What did Sherlock Holmes have to do with fairies?"

Roxanne smiled and shook her head. "Sir Arthur wasn't just about solving mysteries, you know. He also had a fanciful side. Look at the photographs inside."

Carmel flipped through the gray book, where black and white photos were interspersed with heavy text. The subjects of each were young girls in late Edwardian dress, some with what appeared to be fairies hovering nearby, and alighting on their outstretched hands.

"Are these for real? Wait, no, they can't be." Carmel squinted up her eyes. "What's going on here? Why is he writing about these faked photos?"

The English woman laughed. "You caught on fast. Unfortunately, the cardboard cut-outs fooled a lot of people for a long time, even the great writer himself. People see what they want to see, you know. And I guess they wanted to believe so badly that they ignored the evidence in front of their eyes." She took the book back into her hands and pointed to the image facing them. "These photos were created by those young girls, copying from fashion magazines. The 'fairies' were taken from the models," Roxanne continued. "Notice the flapper hair-do's on the fairies? A lot of people at the time didn't."

Carmel sat back. "Amazing," she said. "But I have to ask—what's so special about this book that you carry it with you?"

"I admit when I was eight years old, they fooled me too," the other confessed. "For a couple of years, I was overjoyed to have proof that the fey existed, but then I was devastated to discover these were, after all, faked. I keep this book as a reminder—my first great lesson which has served me well in my career."

"And you've spent your life since then disproving the existence of fairies?" Carmel asked, remembering that Roxanne's lifework involved an anthropological exploration of fairy legends around the world. "Wouldn't you say that's a bit of an extreme reaction?"

The English woman looked at Carmel quizzically through her thick spectacles. "Oh, no," she said. "Quite the opposite. I mean, fairies do exist. They occur in the traditions of most cultures. But they aren't the friendly sprites that are depicted in, say, Disney movies or these photos. The real fey can be quite nasty and territorial—they're thieves, and love to play tricks."

This conversation had taken a turn for the strange. Carmel eyed the woman opposite her warily. "And what sort of evidence do you have that they exist?"

"Not a lot," Roxanne admitted, her eyes intense behind her glasses, talking with passion. "And they take different forms in each culture. I was, however, part of the team that captured the footprints of the Orang Kardil in Northern Sumatra. Some members of our group spotted the creature, but, of course, you don't want to get too close to the Kardil. They hate humans, and are quite bloodthirsty."

Later, walking up the laneway back home, Carmel marvelled at Roxanne's matter-of-fact manner when discussing fairies of the world. She was an odd bird, no doubt about it, but harmless enough. *Quite entertaining even, if you don't mind the weirdness*, she thought. And she did know her way around the kitchen.

The next morning, seated in her dining room office, Carmel's attention was caught by the sounds of people passing by under her window. She glanced up and outside, to see the mayor amid a crowd of people in hiking garb walking down the road towards the bridge.

Curious and curiouser, she thought to herself. *Is the mayor conducting tours of the murder site? Developing a new tourist attraction for the area?* She craned her head to watch.

She could hear the sound of Thomas Ryan's voice holding forth but couldn't make out the words, and his hands were flying around in his expressive manner. It only took her a moment to decide her action.

"I have to see what he's up to now," she said, giving up all hope at working this morning. At the same time, she acknowledged she'd have to move her office to a back room, for she wasn't getting any work done perched up here overlooking the community. There was too much happening in this quiet cove. Which reminded her—she wanted to pick Bridget's brain about Farrell. She grabbed the remains of the pie from the fridge to bring to her friend—a few days old and perhaps a little stale, but she figured Bridget would make short work of it.

From the veranda, Carmel had a perfect view of the bridge and the gates to Clyde's farm. The troop paused at the bridge, where there was much shaking of heads, and then nodding of heads. She could see Ryan talking throughout.

They then turned as one body up the incline to Clyde Farrell's farm. Carmel, her own encounter with Farrell still terrifyingly fresh in her mind, waited with much anticipation to see what would happen next. Which one would the dog go for? Her hopes were on the mayor who, although he'd been friendly enough, was far too focused on his own desires and was the obvious instigator of this Farrell baiting.

There was a pause at the gate. Ryan was clearly pointing out the signs forbidding entry, and then gesturing up the hill. The mountain softened somewhat at Farrell's farm, its rugged rocky clefts mellowing to a slope of grasslands where sheep grazed, then fields of vegetables, before rejoining the line of cliffs overhanging the water. The farm's fence, topped with barbed-wire, ran from the road right to the edge of the cliff—there was no room to maneuver around the structure. It was along this shoreline, Ryan had given Carmel to understand, that the hikers wanted to be free to ramble, to reclaim their right to use historic footpaths.

As if arming themselves for battle, the hikers tightened their backpacks and pulled back their shoulders, and opened the forbidding gate into the farm. They paused, and nothing happened. So they cautiously stepped inside the farm, clustered together, each aiming to be in the middle of the cluster. They were acting just like a herd of sheep sensing danger.

Still nothing happened.

Carmel wondered if Farrell was around. She could hear a barking deep within the farmyard, amid the general farm noises of mooing, bleats and clucking. There seemed to be debate amongst the group whether to close the gate behind them. It would be a dilemma, certainly. Would one leave it open to allow a quick getaway, or would it be wiser to close the gate so as not to anger the farmer more? She would have found herself hard pressed to answer that one.

Once inside the gate (with it firmly shut behind them) the group turned to the left. They walked along the narrow cliff in single file hesitantly at first, then with growing confidence. Soon they had disappeared around the bend behind a clump of juniper clinging to the side of the hill, obviously much cheered.

But where was Clyde? The back of his truck was clearly visible from where she stood. Was he ill or... had the killer struck again? Carmel's heart sank as her imagination set in. She could picture him lying, butchered in his own farmyard, the cows lowing to be milked while the dog howled in anguish for his master.... *No, really, that was stretching it*, she decided. That demon would more likely gnaw through the chain and feed on Clyde's dying body for lunch.

And then the sound of a shotgun ricocheted through the tiny cove, the blast echoing from rock to rock. Then silence reigned.

Until the first hiker came running back along the cliff, sending terror-stricken glances behind him, the others not far behind. Thomas Ryan was the last, his short legs working twice as hard. They fumbled at the gate which they had so thoughtfully closed after entering the farm, losing valuable time as Clyde materialized at the top of the rise. He was shaking his fist at them, the hand that wasn't holding the shotgun, and she could hear his roars from where she stood on the veranda.

They didn't pause to close the gate, nor did they stop for breath at the bridge over the gorge. Farrell banged the entry closed behind the group, still sending curses and blasphemes their way. Not until they saw him disappear back into the farmyard did they slow down and catch their collective breaths, only to abuse Ryan for leading them into such a folly. The group were still complaining as one when they reached Carmel's house at the top of the rise.

"You saw it!" Ryan's eyes alighted on the brunette standing above them on her veranda. "You're a witness too. The man is mad, I tell you!" he called out to Carmel.

Far from being upset, Ryan appeared to be in his glee and scarcely able to contain himself.

"Oh, you'll have to lay charges," he agreed with the lead hiker. "The man almost committed murder again, twice in one week. He's a public menace and needs to be put away."

The group twittered away amongst themselves as they passed her house. Carmel watched until they were once more out of sight past the church. She shook her head, and only then noticed Bridget standing on her own step across the road.

"What was that all about?" she called out to her friend as she left her veranda and came down to the road.

"That," Bridget said. "That was politics in action."

She looked at Carmel's sceptical face and laughed. Eyeing the pie dish in her hands, she invited her into the small house.

The first thing to hit Carmel when she stepped inside Bridget's house were the vivid works of art which covered almost every surface. Ranging in size from small to huge, canvases with bright orange and blue slashes jumped out at the eye. It was only when she chose one to focus on could she make out the subject matter.

"It's Phonse and Sid," she said, amazed that Bridget was able to capture the attitudes of the men with so few charcoal lines. They were standing on the wharf, Phonse's boat recognizable though painted with a single confident stroke of orange. She must have used a wall-painting brush to get such a large sweep. A blue streak in the distance was Bell Island. The larger pieces in the room appeared to be part of a series, all on the orange and blue theme.

"I had no idea you were an artist," Carmel said. "And such a talented one, at that."

Bridget glowed at the praise. "Do you like it?" she asked. "No one around here does, much. Vee says... well... Hey, I have an exhibit coming up next month in town. Will you come?"

"I'd be delighted to."

"This is what I do for fun," Bridget said, encouraged now. "Not much of a living to be made at it, though. Come down and I'll show you the pottery studio."

She led her down a narrow set of stairs, all painted with stars and three-dimensional cubes. It was like walking down into a crazy patched quilt. The basement was a single room carved into the hillside with a wall of granite at the back, the bedrock foundation of the house, all painted white, and the front was floor to ceiling windows looking out over the water. On the sides were numerous shelves holding brightly painted pots and mugs, with a tiny kiln nestled in the corner of the room. A throwing wheel sat in the very center.

After Carmel had shown she was suitably impressed by the set-up and the work, Bridget led her back upstairs and over tea and pie, she told her of the history between Portugal Cove's mayor and St. Jude Without.

"Thomas Ryan, who is, by the way, no relation of mine," Bridget began.

"He's already made that clear," Carmel agreed.

"He wants to turn St. Jude Without into an amusement park," Bridget said, the disgust in her voice evident.

"I thought he wanted an archeological dig and museum. He didn't say anything about a theme park."

"Museum, park, what does he care?" Bridget asked. Between her eyebrows, a vertical line appeared which hadn't been there before. "As long as he can collect taxes on it and have it named after himself, he wouldn't be particular."

"He thinks Clyde killed Peters," Carmel told her, remembering back to the conversation she'd had with him.

Bridget nodded. "That makes sense then. He's trying to prove Farrell is off his rocker, and then finally get him out of the way."

"And he tried to inveigle me as a witness, too," Carmel said.

"Maybe there is something left behind by the Beothuk there," Bridget said, "but if any proof of them is ever found, Clyde would lose his farm. Sure, the government would buy him out so they could do the archaeological digs and make the place into a heritage site, but where would that leave him? Where would he go? That farm is his life."

Carmel related to her the encounter she'd had with Clyde's dog.

"I think Thomas Ryan's the crazy one," Carmel said. "Why would he risk going in that farm and having that dog savage him?"

Bridget laughed, not an amused sound.

"He knew damn well he was quite safe from Clyde's dog," she said, her mouth in a thin line. "You see, years ago when Ryan started all this nonsense, he pulled the same trick. Got a bunch of city yuppies out one day, to 'reclaim the trail.' He thought with a crowd, Farrell wouldn't be able to do anything about it. But he miscalculated that day. Clyde wasn't home. However, his dog was. A different dog. Who bit and severely injured one of them."

She stopped and gazed through the window back up the road to the farmyard. "When Clyde came back that day, they told him what had happened," she said. "He went right out and shot that dog, though it might have been the only creature that ever loved him. He's been heartbroken ever since that day, and he won't let anyone on the farm at all now."

Carmel was appalled. "He shot his own dog? That's cruel. The animal was defending his farm."

"Had to," Bridget replied in a matter of fact tone. "Can't let a dog live who's got a taste for blood, cause he might do it again. Same as if he went after a sheep."

Rural life was harsh, and its ethics severe. From a tradition where life was tenuous at best, the rules for the tribe's survival were strictly enforced by all.

"So Ryan knew Farrell wouldn't set the dog on him," Carmel said, thoughtfully. "Clyde wouldn't risk another dog having to be put down."

"Ryan knew Clyde wouldn't aim to kill with the gun, either," Bridget said. "He's setting up to get rid of Clyde, there's no doubt. Makes me wonder if it was Ryan himself killed Peters, just to cause havoc. He sure as hell didn't want that development up there."

Carmel nodded in agreement, but her mind was still on the death of Clyde's dog. Rural life had a whole different set of values, she was finding out. Killing a beloved dog for the greater good of the community... Could someone have killed Peters, whom no one loved, for the same reason? Again, she wished she had someone with whom to discuss what was on her mind. Bridget was too close to them all—she had this same mindset.

What really bothered her was the question—was Thomas right about Clyde being the murderer?

"Oh, *you're* here," the woman said as she let herself in the kitchen door. Vee wasn't happy to see Carmel in Bridget's small home. "Just on my way to the store, and I thought I'd drop off some fish for you Bridget."

"Thanks, Aunt Vee," Bridget said, taking the plastic bag from Phonse's mom. "Won't you come in?"

The older woman made a face in Carmel's general direction, but graciously accepted the invitation. The omnipresent curlers were back in her hair, Carmel noted.

"Phonse had a good day out there, then?" Bridget asked as she placed the bag in the fridge.

"Fair to middling, I'd say," Vee said. "He works so hard, that boy."

Carmel snorted on her tea, and attempted to turn it into a cough while Mrs. Ryan looked suspiciously at her. She'd seen Phonse 'working hard' on her roof.

At least his mother mellowed out somewhat after Bridget gave her a slice of Carmel's pie. "Pastry's a little stale," she said, wiping up the last of the flakes and juice with her fingers and licking them. "And awfully runny, isn't it? I use tapioca to thicken it myself, that's how Phonse likes it."

Bridget rolled her eyes at Carmel, but was able to turn the conversation away from Mrs. Ryan's son.

"Saw you on the news the other night," Bridget said cautiously.

Mrs. Ryan looked perplexed. "I watched it too. But I never said those things," she said. "At least I might have said them, but I didn't…"

"He was playing with you Aunt Vee," Bridget said. "He edited it to make you look like a fool."

"He seemed so nice," the older woman replied, her face drooping. "And he was interested, y'know?" Carmel could almost feel sympathy for her.

"Never mind that," Bridget soothed her. "He'll get what's coming to him one day. Karma has a way of getting its own back." She told Vee what the two had witnessed that afternoon.

"That Clyde, I wonder he hasn't murdered one of that crowd yet," Vee said, shaking her head. "Do you remember the time he near did away with Melba up there?" she asked Bridget, who frowned back at her. "She up there picking mushrooms from the cow field, like she always done since before he was born, and he chased her off like she was some townie tourist. She cursed him up and down and all around and then you know what happened." She nodded knowingly.

"You don't need to be spreading old foolishness like that now, Aunt Vee," Bridget interjected.

"His cow died," Vee continued as if she hadn't heard her niece. "Up and died, a good cow like that."

"I don't think Melba's words could have killed a cow," Carmel pointed out, trying to lighten the conversation for she could see that Bridget was growing ever more uncomfortable. "There would be a lot more death around if it was that easy."

"Oh, Melba said it wasn't the cursing." Vee's eyes crinkled in malicious merriment. "She claimed it was the fairies done it for her. Crazy old bat. And if anyone could have done in Peters, would be her," she added. "Never fished in her life but she's knows a good bit about butchering, I allows."

"Melba said she knew what happened the night Peters was killed," Carmel said, to steer the subject away, for she could see Bridget was getting increasingly upset across the table.

"Did she now? And did she tell the cops that?"

"No, she told them the opposite," her niece hurried to say, after shooting a dark glance at Carmel. "I think she was just in one of her moods."

"Craziness, more like," Vee spat gleefully.

Mrs. Ryan didn't seem to have a good word for anyone in the small community apart from her son, despite avowing they were all her family. A nastier woman Carmel had yet to meet. She idly played with the idea that Vee herself had offed Peters, but decided against it. She barely had breath to make it up the front steps last night, let alone toss a big burly man over a bridge.

Chapter 9

Carmel awakened the next day to the sound of sirens sounding loud throughout the cove.

Oh God, what now? she wondered, rubbing her eyes as she peered out of the tiny upstairs window just in time to see the white ambulance run past her house. She picked up yesterday's jeans and t-shirt from the floor where she'd left them last night, quickly throwing them on.

She couldn't see anything from her front door. Not a thing but fog—thick white fog trailing its fingers through the trees, obliterating anything further afield than the road.

Did Clyde finally kill a hiker? she wondered as she slipped into her canvas shoes and walked outside. She gave a shiver and turned back to pull a sweatshirt over her head. The morning was chill and damp.

The sirens were off by this time and there was no sign of them on the road, but when she'd almost reached the bridge, she saw movement on Melba's overgrown laneway and fresh tire tracks through the long grass. As she reached the emergency vehicle, lights still flashing, she saw a stretcher being loaded into the back. It held Melba—pale and unmoving under the straps. The old woman must have had a stroke. Carmel's eye could see that she was barely breathing, but there was no sign of blood or injury. Bridget was being held back from scrambling into the back with her by one of the attendants.

"You're best off staying here," he told her, and catching Carmel's eye, indicated for her to join them. "She's too panicky to come with us," he said in a low voice as she approached. "More nuisance than help."

They slammed shut the back of the ambulance. Carmel stood back and let the ambulance back down the narrow lane.

"What happened?" she asked Bridget. Her hippy friend turned with a sob and grabbed her in her arms. "Is she…"

"Almost dead," Bridget replied. "If I hadn't come by, oh my Lord, she was lying there foaming from her mouth, I didn't know what was happening."

She was almost incoherent, so hysterical was she.

"Come on," Carmel said, nudging her back towards Melba's kitchen door, not knowing what else to suggest. "Let's make a cup of tea. Melba wouldn't mind."

They walked in through the back door, straight into the kitchen. The teapot with its cheery crocheted cosy sat on the table. Next to it, a cup lay overturned on the table, the liquid still puddled on the floor beneath it.

"Best not go in there," came Darrow's deep voice behind them. "We'll need to check it out first."

He stood in front of a phalanx of white-suited SOCOs. Their vehicles had drawn up silently after the ambulance left.

"What's going on?" Carmel asked him, bewildered and not a little scared at the sight. "What on earth is happening here?"

"We intercepted the emergency call," he replied, nodding to Bridget. "They're not sure what happened to Melba, but we're treating it as suspicious until proved otherwise. I have to ask you to leave the scene. Come away please."

As he held the door open for them, Carmel noticed the plastic gloves on his hand.

"I didn't touch anything," she said.

"Did you?" he asked Bridget, who stared at him, uncomprehending.

Carmel placed her arm around her friend's shoulder protectively.

"Question her later," she said to him. "She's not fit for it right now."

The two women started to take the path through the woods, but were stopped by a uniformed officer, who pointed them towards the roadway. In light of Peters' recent death, the police were taking this very seriously indeed.

Tea and toast heavily laden with butter and jam helped bring back the colour to Bridget's ashen face. The shock hadn't hurt her appetite, Carmel couldn't help but notice. In time, Darrow had joined them at the kitchen table.

"The only fingerprints we've found in the kitchen are Melba's and yours, Bridget," he said. He was staring hard at her. "Melba kept a pretty clean ship."

"She's old-school. Everything has to be spotless at all times," she said as she continued staring into the dregs of her cup. "But still, I don't understand why you and the police are involved."

"We've not gotten any closer to finding Peters' murderer," he pointed out. "With a lot of heat coming from above, we have to be watchful of anything going on in this cove. Not to mention the media presence."

They all grimaced at that.

"This pressure has helped us get fast results from the lab, at any rate. We were right to act quickly, for she'd been poisoned. It's a good thing you found her when you did, and called for help."

Both women looked up at this news, eyes wide. Poisoned!

"Aconitum can work quickly. Fortunately, she's a large woman and she didn't drink enough of the tea to do her in. Not yet, at any rate. She'll be kept in ICU for the next couple of days. We'll see how she goes."

"You're saying someone poisoned Melba?" Carmel could hardly believe her ears. Yes, she accepted that the police had to investigate anything strange in the cove, so soon after Peters' mysterious murder, but who would poison the old woman? Melba had nothing to do with the development, or politics, or anything as far as Carmel knew.

"That someone could have been Melba herself," he said. "Aconitum is another word for Monkshood, which is growing all around the back of her flowerbeds. She probably took it herself, by accident. The tea pot was full of it."

Darrow went on his way after dropping this bombshell on them.

"I thought it was a stroke," Carmel said, still stunned by the news. "She's an old woman, things happen."

"How could she have mistaken monkshood? She of all people would know it's poisonous." Bridget stood up and looked out at Carmel's own back yard with the overgrown flower beds. The deep blue of the monkshood flowers were gone by now, this late in the season, like many of the perennial flowers, but their drying seed pods towered over all the other plants.

"She gave me mallow tea the other day," Carmel said. "Could she have confused the leaves?" All the while she was thinking that it could so easily have been herself found frothing and twitching from the accidental poisoning.

"The leaves look a bit alike," Bridget said, doubt showing on her face. "They're both sort of frondy, with long fingers of leaf, but even without the flowers to identify them, mallow is so much shorter that it's not something Melba would ever mistake."

Carmel hesitated before she asked. "Has she seemed alright to you—mentally, I mean? You know, she's not getting funny in the head, forgetful, anything you've noticed lately?"

She was thinking back on her previous meetings with the old woman, who seemed to slip from normal to la-la in a matter of seconds. Her grasp on reality didn't seem to be all there at times. Perhaps during one of those moments, Melba had harvested the monkshood leaves for her morning tea, not realizing that she might be signing her own death warrant.

Bridget turned at her now, her guard up. "Are you suggesting she's crazy?"

"Not insane, no. But there was all her talk about the fairies. She spoke like they were real, like they were her friends or something. Face it, Bridget, that's not quite normal."

The two stared each other down over the kitchen table. Bridget was the first to break the contact.

"Well," she said, picking up her bag and giving a flick of her dark red hair. "That depends on what your definition of normal is."

"But if it wasn't Melba herself who made the mistake, then…"

Bridget hesitated in her exit and didn't meet her gaze.

"You know what it must mean," Carmel said. "A deliberate poisoning. She said she saw something the night Peters died."

"And you told Aunt Vee," Bridget replied with sagging shoulders. "Which means that the whole community knew by supper time. Maybe even the TV reporters. I saw her up talking with Gerald Smythe, even after what he did to her on his show." She turned again to leave.

"Stupid, stupid woman," Bridget muttered. Carmel wasn't sure if she meant Vee or herself.

Carmel let her friend go on her way. She herself remained motionless and lost in thought. Yes, she had told Vee that Melba claimed to know something about Peters' murder. The woman would certainly have loved to pass that gossip on. She recalled the younger woman's reaction when Melba had gleefully inferred she knew who the killer was. Could Bridget herself have administered the poison?

There was no way, simply no way, that Bridget could have offed Peters that stormy night. The rain had already been lashing down when they left the bar, and Darrow had said the murder had to have happened just as it started. But Bridget could be protecting someone else, and now deeply regretting what she'd done.

Despite the excitement of the early morning, Carmel had managed to set aside the whole chunk of time between morning and late afternoon for work. She wasn't writing about Bell Island this week after her unproductive trip out there with Phonse, but there was still lots of material from her previous forays on islands down the shore and in other bays. Satisfied that her work was complete for the day, Carmel gave a deep stretch to her back, twisting her head, listening to the crunching of her spinal cord. *I should really make time to pick up my yoga practice,* she thought.

As she walked towards the kitchen, she mentally checked off her to-do list for the next day, which included several errands in the city. With the exception of her jaunts into Portugal Cove to the south, she'd had no contact with the outside world, not even a trip to St. John's in the past few days since she'd arrived, and she realized she was feeling just the tiniest bit claustrophobic. Not, of course, the terrifying claustrophobia she felt in small enclosed places and in her nightmares, but there was a definite feeling that she needed to see people and traffic, stretch her horizon a little. *Perhaps this is what happened in the cove*, she thought idly, *it sucks you in to its cozy dramas so the rest of life drifted off and passes by like a dream.* The mountain wove its protective spell so that not only could it pass under the radar of the larger world, but the residents became caught up in the web and couldn't leave. She laughed and shook her head, thinking maybe she should try her hand at writing fiction.

The smell of smoke inside the house was the first thing to alert her that something was amiss, and then she noticed the wet plastic bag sitting in the sink. One flat silver eye glinted out at her from glistening white folds of plastic, and her own eyes followed the line of drips on the floor. Phonse beamed at her from the old oak table where he'd made himself quite at home with beer from her fridge and the remains of last night's pizza.

"You need to get an ashtray," he informed her genially. He'd used her favourite saucer with the deep red roses to extinguish the butt.

"You need take that outside," she said, screwing up her nose at the stink and fanning her face. She grabbed paper towels from the roll and wiped up the trail of drips from the bag, stopping when she reached the sink.

"What's this?" She poked her finger into the bag, lifting up a flap of plastic.

"Thought you'd like a good feed of fresh fish. Was out on the boat today."

"Nice. But it's… it's still a fish." In her daydream of frying up the fresh catches from local sources, the fish had been handed to her in civilised fillets. This large cod didn't have any bits missing, and she wasn't quite sure how it could morph into an edible meal.

"You never gutted a fish before?" His brilliant blue eyes were looking at her suspiciously, as if she'd said she'd never watched television or used a computer.

"I'm a writer. What do you think?"

He considered this. "Roxanne's a writer, or something. She handled it no problem."

The sturdy and efficient Roxanne would no doubt make short work of the fish, Carmel was sure. The woman could probably take down a bull moose in rutting season bare-handed and have it prepared for roasting to feed the village in an hour.

She was about to tell him to remove the offending fish with its baleful staring eye, when he generously offered to do the dirty work himself. He found the knife quickly in the back of a drawer, and she watched the muscles in his strong forearms as, with a minimum sequence of actions, the fish was gutted, cleaned and ready for the pan. He put the bowl of non-fillet fishy bits out the back door where Hank had appeared on cue.

"Oh, I forgot about the cat," Carmel said, watching him noisily attacking the bowl through the screen door. "I'll have to look after him while Melba's in the hospital. That is, if she doesn't…"

"Hank'll be okay. Just leave a bit of food out for him. We all do," Phonse said, looking over her shoulder. His arm grazed her and she felt the electric shiver as the warmth of his skin touched the fine hairs of her own arm. As if knowing the effect he was having on her and teasing her, he draped himself over her and breathed in deep the smell of her curls.

"Now, missus," his deep voice said in her ear. She could feel the rumbling through his chest and her own back. Damn. A blush was creeping up over her chest and neck as she could feel her nipples responding against her will. "How's about a fry-up of potatoes with that?"

He withdrew from her body, leaving the evening air cool on her back.

"Can you reach me another beer?" Phonse asked as he sprawled himself back at the table.

She found herself complying. *Well, really*, she explained to herself, *what was the harm?* He had provided the fish, and cleaned and filleted it for her too. Carmel opened herself a beer while she rifled through her cookery magazines for a simple fish recipe and sauce, then chopped the potatoes ready for the pan.

"Not bad," he said, letting out a polite belch as he pushed the empty plate away and tipped back his chair. "You haven't got the light touch with panfry that Mudder has, but not bad at all. She always says that only bad cooks use sauces to cover up bad cooking, but that was alright, I suppose."

Carmel fumed a little as she washed the dishes and left them to drip-dry on their own. She had thought he might offer to help dry, at least, but he seemed content to watch the news on her TV as she worked at cleaning the fishy mess and he worked his way through her beer. She was beginning to suspect that this was the 'traditional' behaviour that Bridget had tried to warn her about.

Gerald Smythe's boyish grin filled the small screen as he talked about the cove.

"Still no action from police in the terrible murder of Eric Peters," he noted. "And a strange new twist has come to light." He leaned closer to the camera, almost salivating in his glee.

"The local witch has been found poisoned in her home," he told his audience, eyes wide in wonder. "That's right, the witch of St. Jude Without, the one who poisoned her neighbour's cow, has been given a taste of her own medicine."

The screen flashed back to his interview with Mrs. Ryan and her bit about the fairies. Phonse hooted with laughter. His blue eyes danced to Carmel.

"There's Mudder, making a fool of herself," he said, grinning. "That Smythe got her wrapped around his little finger."

"I think he's the one making a fool of her." Carmel dried her hands on a dishtowel.

"Was it the fairies?" Smythe was now asking his listeners. "Are we talking supernatural activity in this forgotten cove? The last holdout of the little people?"

Phonse's laughter was quickly dropped as he straightened in his chair and looked on with growing concern.

"Maybe I can help solve this mystery." Smythe now nodded to the camera. "Tomorrow night, under the light of the full moon, I suggest a hunt for the elusive little people. Stay tuned." The screen cut to ads.

"Geez," Phonse said. "There's no need for all this. He's going to ruin the place."

Carmel couldn't believe her ears. Was Phonse seriously talking about the existence of fairies?

"What's he going to ruin?" she asked him cautiously. He turned to look at her, his eyes narrowed.

"Our privacy," he replied at last. "We're going to have all types of camera crews and New Agers and weirdoes out tramping round the woods and the cove. Going to ruin the place. Tomorrow night of all times."

Carmel's fridge had run out of beer so Phonse headed over to the old church, inviting her to join him almost as an afterthought. There she found Bridget and Roxanne and shared with them Smythe's latest gambit, along with beer and potato chips. She also mentioned in passing Phonse's abrupt reaction to Smythe's announcement of his plans.

The fisherman himself was huddled in conference with Sid, a frown wrinkling his brow as he gesticulated in a worried fashion. Sid, expressionless as always, laid a hand on his shoulder and gave a short nod before returning to his biker friends.

"So why did he say, 'tomorrow of all nights?'" Carmel asked Bridget, still curious as to Phonse's strange reaction.

Bridget didn't meet her eyes as she shrugged. "Who knows?"

She finally looked up and smiled weakly. "Maybe they're planning a party in the woods and don't want the company. You know, getting back to their teenage roots. That crowd haven't grown up yet in case you haven't noticed." She shrugged again as she wandered away to the bar.

Carmel turned to Roxanne. "Do you have any idea what's going on?" she asked the other woman, getting exasperated.

Roxanne considered. "I don't know about the woods," she said, "but I'd keep a close eye on the water if you want the answer. Tomorrow's a full moon, right?"

"That's what Smythe said," Carmel replied, remembering the news report.

Roxanne nodded thoughtfully. "And what happens under a full moon?" she asked, a small smile playing on her face.

"Werewolves?" Carmel asked back, trying to think. "Witches dancing? Though the so-called witch is in the ICU so I don't think she'll be doing much of that."

"What else?"

"Don't tell me this story of fairies is true," Carmel said. "I know you're the expert on fairy-lore, but seriously? Besides, I thought fairies didn't like salt water."

Wait, she thought, reaching back through her mind to the historical books she'd read years ago. Water. Full moon. *Smugglers* moon.

"What are they smuggling?" she asked tersely even as her eye fell on the beer in her tankard.

"I don't know that for a fact," Roxanne replied. "But I'm sure it's harmless. You've got the perfect vantage point." A gleam came in her eye. "Why don't you keep watch tomorrow night? Your front veranda will give you the best seat for watching the action."

Carmel thought about that later, sitting on her back step for a cigarette before turning in for the night. Smuggling, eh? That would go a long way to answering some questions about the strange attitudes she'd encountered in the cove. Phonse was a fisherman, but she didn't see him go out on the water much, and never saw him hauling fish off in his battered truck. He just dropped off bags of cod for the locals, herself included. He had to be supplementing his income somehow.

And the bar—how obvious was it when she thought about it in this new light? Of course Sid didn't want to attract too much business. The beer was probably smuggled in from Quebec, and the bar was a front for him and his biker companions, a way to launder their money while the real bucks were coming in via deliveries from Phonse's boat. Naturally, all the residents of the community must be in on it, and that's why they wanted to protect the privacy of the little cove. Too many prying eyes would ruin the nice sideline they'd all set up. Even Mrs. Ryan and Clyde must be in on it she realized now. Did Clyde stash the loot in one of his outbuildings? Was that why he had the scary dog and fired his gun off so freely? Perhaps he didn't care about the trail at all, he just didn't want people snooping on his land.

With a sinking heart, she understood the implications of this new line of thought. This would mean that Peters' death was a community affair.

It takes a village... she thought. With everyone covering up for each other, the murder could have been a group effort. Of course, they didn't want Peters coming in and opening up the cove, making the wharf into an exclusive marina, taking away their livelihoods. Where would they land their smuggled goods? The cove as it was, was perfect for their operations. No streetlights and a closely-guarded secret among the extended family.

And if the whole cove was involved in the smuggling and murder, then Bridget was too. Did she poison Melba to stop the old woman from talking out of turn, to save the others? Remembering back on the story of Farrell's other dog, she shivered. The almost full moon darkened above as clouds raced over it.

Carmel started as she became aware of tiny flickering lights off in the woods again, over by the old graveyard. "Fireflies," she at last decided. "Didn't think we had them here on the island." There were no kids shouting or playing, or even partying and other dark deeds. All was dead silent.

She watched the insects dancing, furiously, their lights winking on and off as if flashing messages, uncomfortably like a warning to her. But she didn't feel they were telling her to leave the cove and run for safety and sanity back in the twenty-first century of the larger city. She was not getting a sensation of impending danger or doom. No, these tiny lights were flashing like a plea for help, their desperation evident in the intensity of their firing.

Carmel resolutely turned her back on them, shaking her head at the way her imagination was firing these days. Placing the now-dry dishes back in the cupboards, her eye was caught by the red book laying on the counter. She knew she hadn't touched it since putting it back on the shelf last night—was Phonse playing tricks on her? She wouldn't put it past him. Shaking her head, she refused to pick the horrible dirty thing up again. Pirates indeed.

The image on the book cover must have ingrained itself on her retina, for in the split second as she was switching off the light, she could have sworn she saw the reflection of a man with a wide-brimmed hat, feather and all, in the window. She realized she too was now part of the cove, surely, for she was getting as crazy as the rest of them.

Chapter 10

The morning dawned slowly, the low clouds lifting
only to reveal fingers of thick sea fog clinging to the
cove and the point, blanketing the meadows and
shoreline as if clinging to secrets lurking deep within.
From her window, Carmel could see through the haze
to the thrusting line of Bell Island's cliffs in the
distance—yet in the foreground, nothing of the point of
land beyond her window, nothing of the wharf. All was
smothered beneath the sullen gray fog.

Doesn't bode well for smuggling activities this
evening, she thought, just a little relieved, yet at the
same time she knew she'd be watching out anyway.
Yes, she was caught up in the dramas of the small cove
which was her new home.

And finally she made it to the city to do what she'd
been neglecting for too long. Her errands done, she
lingered in the downtown, breathing in the lightly
dieseled air of Water Street and felt comfort in the press
of people all around her. The sun had dissipated the fog
on this side of the mountain, the fresh breeze off the
Atlantic dispersing the last of the clouds. Blue sky
peeked over the tall buildings—not skyscrapers, no—
but close enough together to block the sun on the late
August morning. Down past the bakery, she saw a
familiar media van, and Veronica Dourley lounging
against it, her long thin legs now encased in shimmery
silk tights. Summer was quickly drawing to a close, and
with the advent of the cooler air and the start of the
university semester, the George Street nightly riots had

also wound down. Only shards of glass glinting in the gutters and the single boarded window on the wool store remained as signs of the inexplicable violence that had occurred in this relatively peaceful city.

She stopped at the Portugal Cove post office on her way home, one of the last little community gathering places left still standing during this Conservative political regime. Soon it too would go, no doubt, to be replaced by steel boxes out in the open, for people to dash over to in the rain to grab their mail and run off again before getting wet—no time to stand and linger and talk about the latest treacheries committed by all levels of the elected governments. Among fliers, bills and an assortment of correspondence, Carmel found a long-awaited envelope in her box.

"The contract!" Finally, what she'd been hoping for had come through. She sat on the bench outside the post office to read it. Yes, they'd accepted her query and were interested in a five-part series, once a month, for this prestigious travel magazine, on the little known mysteries of islands around the world, with a possible extension depending on the popularity of the regular pieces. They wanted St. Kitt's; they wanted Bermuda, Santorini and even Taiwan. The fifth, they suggested, might be the Orkney Islands off the north coast of Scotland, a hitherto unexplored territory for her but one which was high on her bucket list. She kissed the paper, signed it and dropped it back on its way through the slot of the mailbox.

Once home, Carmel set herself to outlining her ideas for her new commission—all thoughts of murder, smuggling and fairies gone from her mind. She forgot about the cove completely as she lost herself in the work to be done and the travel plans to be made. Although she'd spent extended periods of time on most of the islands, she easily won the argument with herself that—yes—she needed to revisit these familiar lands and friends still living there.

Still looking ahead to her future travels, she flicked through the rest of the takings from her post office box. The bills could be dealt with later, the fliers went straight to the recycling bag. One envelope remained— a thick cream vellum, embossed with the name of a local lawyer's office.

This was intriguing, and she wasted no time ripping it open. The way her luck was going so far today, perhaps it was notice of an inheritance from a long-lost branch of her small family, she laughed to herself.

But it was better, in a way. A lot better, in that it was a lot more real. She'd forgotten that when she'd accepted the lease on the house, she had casually asked the agent if there was any possibility that she could buy the house, as the landlord had moved south to America. Her inquiry must have been passed on, for she now had an answer.

"We are happy to inform you," the letter read, "that the owner of the property located at civic address #306 North Point Road Extension in the community of St. Jude Without has, after careful consultation with other interested parties, agreed to the sale of said property to you." This was followed by a jumble of legal jargon— the here-to's and not-withstandings, but the gist of the letter stated the sum the house was being offered for. A quick calculation of present mortgage rates, what she could use as down payment, and how much she could afford for a monthly payment, and Carmel realized the house could be hers. She could have a permanent home base.

So energized was she by her day so far that after she'd broken off for lunch, Carmel tackled the last of the patiently waiting unpacked boxes in the parlor. When those were straightened, she found that even that hadn't tired her humming energy, and so decided to give the place a good scrub down and rearrangement to truly make this outwardly ugly house her own—on the inside at any rate. It was far too late in the year to tackle the jungle outside, and besides, she rather liked the privacy offered by the wild hedge between her and the church.

A hermit needs some sort of privacy, after all, she thought ruefully. *Privacy and secrets. I really fit into this cove, don't I?*

Oh, the cobwebs she knocked down, and the dust that she collected on her micro-fiber cloth. She could hardly believe she hadn't noticed any of it before. All the clutter that inevitably gathers on table tops and mantel was swept away and tucked away, to be dealt with another day. The windows shone and the lemon smell of cleaner lifted her heart further if that was possible.

A polite yet firm knock at the front door caused her to look up. The people of the cove didn't knock; they just walked right in as she was now well aware. Brushing the curls out of her eyes, and adjusting her top, she let her visitor in.

"Roxanne," she said warmly. "Forgive the mess I'm in."

"Looks like you're busy," the Englishwoman said. "Need a hand?"

"Tell you what, you put on the kettle while I move this sofa." It *had* to go beneath the window and she was determined to get it there before stopping her work, but the solid wooden couch was not budging from the place it had stood for years, no matter how much she pushed and pulled at it.

Roxanne laughed at her efforts. "Tell you what—I'll move the sofa, you boil the kettle."

Roxanne squatted down and with one quick shove the sofa obediently slid into place, centered directly under the window.

"How'd you do that?" Carmel asked in wonder. "You're shorter than me."

"Mind over matter," Roxanne replied. "Besides, I'm strong as an ox, you know."

"I have news," Carmel said, her face glowing as she showed her the two important letters she'd received.

"I'm delighted for you," Roxanne said, her expression thoughtful. "It's great about the contract. However, are you really wanting to take on this house permanently, with the shape it's in?"

The leaky roof. The rotted boards of the veranda. The non-existent paint on the ocean side of the clapboard siding. Carmel's exultant mood faded fast as she was reminded of the list of repairs needed. "There's that, of course," she said slowly. She thought some more, but decided quickly. "Doesn't matter. I'm sure it's all do-able. The house has stood for two hundred years. It can hold out and I'll do all the renovations when I can."

Roxanne looked at her sceptically. "You might want to think harder about what you're letting yourself in for," she advised. "And just what does the lawyer mean when he says he 'consulted interested parties'?"

Carmel looked at the letter again. "I'm not really sure," she replied. "Perhaps he asked the residents of the Cove if they wanted me as a neighbour?" This last was said in a joking manner, but Roxanne continued to look a little put out.

"It's probably got to do with legal-speak, you know, possible next of kin, and stuff like that," Carmel assured her. She felt like she was trying to smooth ruffled feathers but not quite sure why she was doing so. "Hey, how about that tea?"

Over the inevitable brew and a fresh tin of cookies, the English woman again brought up the prospect of the smuggling.

"What makes you think anyone in the cove is involved in smuggling?" Carmel asked, curious.

"I've been here a few months, and I've seen some strange things going on, late at night on the water," Roxanne told her. "I'm a light sleeper sometimes, and can be up at all hours. Boats going to and fro in the dark, meeting other craft out on the sea, mostly out past Farrell's farm. There."

She pointed past the low cliffs of the old farmland, out where the land sloped more gently to the sea. "Being down on the point, I have a wider view. They can't be seen by most of the cove, but it's close enough for a quick hop out there with no one else the wiser. Now, when I say 'the cove,' I admit I don't know who all is involved," Roxanne continued in a confidential manner. "But someone's taking Phonse's boat, and there's movement between the church and the wharf. That's all I'm saying."

"They're taking an awful chance, aren't they?" Carmel said, already knowing where her sympathies lay. She recalled how upset Phonse had been last night when he heard Smythe would be knocking around the cove that evening, no doubt making a nuisance of himself. The news reporter wouldn't find any evidence of fairies, but there was a good chance he'd see the activity on the water and wonder about it. And he'd have his camera at the ready, too, to catch it all on film and use the footage to make another sensational story about the cove. "Smythe is going to be hanging around tonight."

"He'll be bumbling around up in the woods," Roxanne said, dismissing the reporter. "I wouldn't worry for the smugglers."

She stood up to take her leave. "Besides," she continued. "They're big lads—all of them—and can take care of themselves. And Smythe, if necessary."

"Now, don't forget to watch for smugglers this evening," she reminded Carmel. "It's not often you'll get a chance to see something like this. You'll need to keep a close eye out the front."

The bikers returned that afternoon, the entire neighborhood rent by the sound of their air-splitting motors, the roar rolling down to the point and then out to sea. Single file, they came up the North Point Road at a sedate pace, yet sounding for all the world like a whole cavalcade of demons descending from the mountain above. Carmel shivered as she watched them pull up to the old church and cut their engines. *It must be true, then*, she thought, *about the smuggling, or why would they be back?* The police were finished with their investigations, at least at the scene of the murder, and were nowhere to be seen. It was safe for the bikers to return to their nefarious nocturnal activities.

Except the police presence was not quite gone yet, she found. Darrow dropped in on her again, his face grim.

"I have a feeling there might be strange activities happening this evening," he said. "Best to stay within your home and not get involved."

"Strange activities?" she echoed. *How much did he know?* Carmel wondered. Was he talking about Smythe's foolish plan to traipse through the woods after dark, looking for non-existent little people in his bid to make more fun of the inhabitants of the cove? Or did Darrow know about the smuggling? She couldn't ask, because, it occurred to her, that maybe the police had no inkling as to what the bikers were up to. Them, she didn't care so much about. They were an unkempt group whose noisy motorcycles ruined her peace in this tiny community. But Phonse was involved, somehow, if only by the use of his boat, and that was another matter. Even though the man drove her crazy with his ways, and his mother was horrible, and—yes—he could be a bit of a pig in his treatment of women, still that physical attraction, her reaction to his physical presence, prevented her from seeing him as a total villain. Let's face it, he was a nice guy when she wasn't falling all over him. He already had 'form' with the police, and she didn't want to be the cause of him getting into more trouble.

She found Darrow watching her, a curious look on his face.

"Yes, stay home tonight." She nodded to show she was on top of it. "Got it."

One of his eyebrows quirked up in question. He wasn't fooled. He knew there was something she wasn't saying, and she knew he knew, and that he recognized this also. It was a stand-off.

"I got great news today," she began to babble, as an excuse to break the staring contest. "My magazine wants me to write a series of articles on islands all over the world. I've been praying for this, and it's finally happened."

His brow cleared. "That's wonderful news," he said, then hesitated. "Are these islands you've already visited?"

"Most of them, yes," she replied. "But I'll need to go back again, of course. It's going to involve a lot more travel. It's good to refresh my memories."

"But how much travelling?"

She took a moment to think. "A lot over the next few months. These islands are scattered all over the world. And, of course, I haven't yet been to the Orkneys—so I'd like to spend as much time as I possibly can there, to really get the feel of it."

"I could give you some contacts for those isles," he said. "I still have family there."

"This day just keeps getting better," she replied, a wide grin breaking out on her face.

"It'll be expensive to stay any amount of time there," he said, "however, my cousin does have a holiday villa on the main island which, if you go in the off-season, can be had for a good price, especially if you're staying any amount of time."

She nodded. "That's how I work," she said with a dreamy smile. "I need to take time, drink coffee on the square every morning, get to know the people living there. That's how to find what a place is really about, and find the little known secrets I can write about."

"Infiltrate, you mean?" he said. "Like police work, in a way."

She laughed, but a slight frown passed over his face.

"Will you be leaving, then? Giving up the lease on this house?"

"That's another part of this wonderful news day," she said, pure pleasure coloring her voice. "Frank Ryan is offering to sell me the house. I've worked it out—by getting a room-mate in, I could afford to pay the mortgage, so I'll have a home base to return to in between assignments." The more she thought about it, the more the idea appealed. Everything she'd originally liked about this house still held—the proximity to the city, the view and closeness of the ocean, and the quiet of the tiny community. Despite the murder, the bikers, and Melba's poisoning, she liked living here and the house felt welcoming, if a house could do that. She liked Bridget, and, of course, there was Phonse.

"And I already have someone to share with," she said. "Roxanne will probably take it on—she'd mentioned she had wanted to rent this house but the timing wasn't right, and also her house is promised to someone else in mid-September. I know she likes the view from here."

Noticing the slight frown deepening on his face, she paused. "You're not looking to move in then, are you? Probably a bit of a move down the social scale, wouldn't you say?" She blushed when she realized how flirtatious this sounded. It hadn't been her intention.

"God no, woman," he said, not bothering to hide his disgust at the idea, then relented. "Not sure your neighbors would be too happy having a cop as a neighbour here."

She agreed, both relieved and a little put-out that he had ignored the inadvertent innuendo.

"I'm glad you won't be leaving the area altogether," he said. He kept his gaze on the horizon, not meeting her eye. "I'd quite miss our chats."

"Sorry I haven't found out too much for you," she said. "Every time I think I know who may have killed Peters, something happens to prove me wrong. I'm so confused. I can't really see that it was someone local at all. I mean, yes, any of them could have had the opportunity, and maybe there was more than one person involved. My money is still on Mayor Ryan from Portugal Cove; he seems to be the most active person around here in getting what he wants." She was referring, of course, to his visit to Farrell's farm.

Darrow at last turned his warm brown eyes on her again, this time the smile crinkling through the sadness that lurked around the edges.

"Oh, yes, your detective work," he said. She could have sworn there was a patronizing note in his voice. Really? Her hackles began to rise. "Well, I wouldn't worry too much about it," he continued. "If the entire RNC police detachment can't finger the murderer, I wouldn't expect you to do it."

He rose to leave. "But please, remember my warning. I came to tell you that I'd rather you stayed in your house tonight and not get involved in any of the activity you might see happening outside. It may be dangerous."

As they moved towards the front door, Darrow was on the point of leaving when his glance fell on the now empty and polished mantel in the parlour. She followed his gaze, only just then realizing with a guilty start that in her cleaning fit the other day, she'd absentmindedly removed Ruscan's photo and tidied it away with the clutter. The frame was now lying behind the door of the built-in cabinet to the side of the fireplace. Darrow's gaze left the mantel and met hers.

She let him go without saying a word, so annoyed was she by this time. *Of all the patriarchal jerks*, she thought furiously. Carmel had thought he'd really wanted her input on the residents of the cove, but he was just being a ... jerk. Just an excuse to chat her up, huh? What an arse. And how pathetic that she couldn't even come up with a better, more scathing term than *jerk*. Was he ordering her to stay in her house this evening? She'd show him, no one ordered Carmel McAlistair to stay home when there was action happening.

Of course, she wasn't planning to get involved or interfere with the smugglers. Hell, they might even have guns on them. Were the bikers related to the mafia? She'd heard recently that all drug activity in the entire country could be traced back to Hell's Angels and other biker gangs. So, no, perhaps she didn't want to go out in it, after all. But, it was her choice, and not because Darrow was telling her not to. At any rate, she vowed, she was going to sit on her veranda and watch, and there was nothing he could do about that.

She banged around in her kitchen, chopping vegetables with a vengeance, and generally taking her new found bad mood out on the dishes when the back door swung open. Phonse's head poked round.

"What's for supper?"

"What's it to you?"

"Just asking," he said, affronted. "Geez, what's eating you?"

"Supper is salad," she said. "You won't like it. And there's no beer left."

"That's okay. I brought my own," he said as he entered, twisting the cap off the single bottle in his hand. "And you're right. I don't eat vegetables. Mom'll have a real meal cooked, one with meat. How can you call salad a meal? You don't even eat any bread with it."

He frowned at the bowl full of luscious red tomatoes, spinach and berries.

"By the way, you got fruit in it. That's just weird, that is. Berries go in pie."

"Why is everyone in this cove so concerned with food?" Carmel burst out, taking her annoyance out on Phonse just because he was there. And because he was plenty annoying in himself. "All you guys ever seem to do is eat. Every time people get together, there's food involved. It's eat, eat, eat all the time."

He gave little reaction as if he'd already tuned her out. She took a bowl out of the cupboard and slammed it on the counter. "Except with you, it's eat, drink, drink, eat, drink."

His skin was as thick as an oilskin and just as impermeable. With a shrug, Phonse turned on the TV and swung his leg over the chair. "You got to watch this. I'm on TV."

Not another mockumentary of the cove, she thought wearily. "Smythe's on the other channel."

He hooted with laughter. "That idiot mainlander? Nah, this is on the real news, with Ronnie."

"Veronica Dourley? You're on a first-name basis with her now, I see. What's she interviewing you about?" She desperately wanted to hold onto her bad mood, but curiosity made her leave her salad makings to watch.

"Not as such," he said, imparting absolutely no information whatsoever in that maddening way of his.

"Why don't you get your satellite fixed?" he asked. "This is terrible reception."

Fortunately, it was easy to hold on to a bad mood with Phonse around. "Why didn't you fix it the other day when you were up on the roof?"

"I was mending your roof." he turned away from the screen long enough to give her an incredulous stare. "You can't expect me to do everything, woman." He turned back to the TV. "Oh, shush," he said waving his hand at her. "Here she is."

The snow queen beauty of the evening news cast her icy eye into the camera from behind her desk and deigned to share her story with viewers.

"While other local media were quick to turn their coverage of the terrible murder of Eric Peters into a sensational circus, I have been exploring into the deeper picture. In light of the recent riots on George Street against the government's controversial plans for hydro-electric development and the—shall we say—reluctance of police to find the culprit, I have…"

While she was talking, the back screen changed from pictures of some bars on George Street, file footage of Peters and his brother, then a clip of Veronica outside Sid's church. She was talking up to Phonse, twirling her hair and giggling, and yes, simpering. God, it was a scary sight. The ice queen had been struck by Phonse's good looks and masculine charm, and was fast melting into goo. He was grinning into the camera lens, and waving.

"What the...?" Veronica cut off her explanation as she looked up and saw the screen.

"Turn that off!" she hissed. Carmel could hear the guffaws of the crew behind the camera. "I'll get your asses fired. Let's have some professionalism here, please."

She glared at the lens as she tried to rearrange her expression. "In other news..."

Phonse's smile split his face as he turned down the sound.

"That's it?"

"Not bad, eh?"

"That wasn't an interview."

"Yes, it was. You saw her there, talking to me."

"But when you said 'interview,' I assumed she was getting your opinion, or you had something worth repeating on camera, or... oh forget it."

"Yeah, she was just sluttin' around," he agreed. "Wasn't a proper talk. But I was never on TV before, so I asked the guys to play that shot."

Carmel assumed they complied with his request for the sole joy of showing Veronica in a ridiculous light. It must be hard to work with that demanding cold bitch, and they had to take their fun where they could. Despite Phonse's irritating ways, she had to laugh.

Phonse looked back at her, delighted with her change of heart and as eager as a puppy. "Some handsome bastard, wha?"

For the love of God, she thought, *the man is incorrigible.* Carmel took the damp dish towel and began to flick it at him.

"Get out! Get out of my house! Go back to your mother!"

Laughing now too, he ducked his head and ran off through the still open door.

Determined not to miss a thing that night, she set out to the old church next door to see what was happening. The bar was no more full, and no less full than normal. It looked like a typical evening at Sid's. The usual crowd occupied their usual spots—almost everybody in the cove was there, except for Vee Ryan and Ida, of course. And Roxanne was nowhere to be seen either, but she didn't really count. There seemed to be nothing out of the ordinary, on this night of the full moon.

Yet, something was different, and Carmel struggled to put her finger on it. The music was a little quieter, likewise the patrons. It was not one of the church's more rowdy nights. But there was something more, something in the way the bikers glanced over their shoulders, and how Sid stood solitary at the altar with his arms crossed. It was as if the whole bar was waiting. Was this just her overactive imagination at work again?

She nodded to Bridget.

"Any word on Melba?"

The red head turned a mournful look on her.

"Nothing yet. Still in ICU." Bridget sighed and looked back down at her beer.

Again, Carmel wondered if it was simply Bridget's worry about the old woman that made her so silent, or was there something more on her mind? She looked around the small church again.

Only Phonse seemed unaffected by any atmosphere, lording it over the pool players as he boasted about his television appearance. But apart from asking if he'd gone to Bell Island with Veronica, they weren't paying him much heed.

There was no sign of Smythe yet, Carmel noted as she glanced out the south-facing windows. Perhaps he'd given up on his idea of a fairy hunt in the full moon, though God only knew what that would have entailed. There'd been no signs of his usual van and crew outside, only the gaggle of teens smoking and surreptitiously drinking out of bottles on the boulders outside the bar.

Darrow had warned her to stay in tonight, but hadn't said why. Roxanne had hinted there was to be smuggling activity to watch. The police must know something was afoot. Should she warn Phonse? She wished she'd thought to mention it to him when he was over earlier, but she'd been still smarting from the policeman's attitude. Carmel wasn't sure that there actually was any nefarious activity planned by the fisherman. What a dilemma. She didn't want to approach Phonse. What if she were wrong? Would he be outraged that she thought he was a criminal? Or would he laugh it off?

But Bridget was close to him. Bridget would pass the message on if she thought it was necessary.

"The police think something's happening here in the cove tonight," she told her in a low voice.

Bridget let her gaze pass slowly over the crowd in the bar. "If they think this is something, they need to get a life."

"No, I mean, they're watching out for something," Carmel said. "I was specifically warned to stay inside tonight, and not get involved in anything."

"So why aren't you home?" Bridget asked into her beer.

She could shake the woman, she really could. Perhaps if she came straight out, it would bring Bridget out of her mournful mood and get her to pay attention to the world around her.

"Look, I don't know, but if Phonse is planning anything tonight, I need you to pass on a warning to him," Carmel hissed in Bridget's ear.

The red head looked over to her cousin and sniffed. "Him? If this is about his fishing license not being renewed, Carmel, the cops don't care about that. That's federal jurisdiction. Don't you know anything?"

"Would you at least tell him? Let him know what I said?"

Bridget shrugged. Frustrated by now, Carmel sighed and felt she'd done her part, and decided to leave the cove residents to their own devices. If they were smuggling and got caught, well, it was on their own heads. Darrow was right, best not to get involved.

At 10:15, Sid flashed the lights around his altar, his unspoken request for people to drink up and leave. Early for him, yes, but then his business didn't keep regular hours so there was really nothing strange in that.

Having finished her own beer, she left. Bridget made no motion to join her and barely nodded a good-bye. Once home, Carmel prepared for her vigil by pouring herself a glass of chilled white wine and donning her warmest sweat shirt to sit out on the veranda, turning off all lights in her house. The moon was rising from the mountain behind her in the east, casting shadows, and she would be close to invisible sitting on her darkened porch. The road in front of her was clearly lit up by the light from the harvest moon.

Dark shadows passed in ones and twos along the road as the bar began to empty. There was Phonse, leaving Bridget at her gate as he walked down the laneway. She hoped Bridget had had the sense to pass on her message, if indeed it was relevant. Shortly after she saw Phonse's kitchen door open to let him in—and not too much later—the light in the cottage winked out, leaving it too in darkness. Casting her eye further along the shore to Roxanne's cottage, Carmel saw it was already a dark spot in the landscape. Was Roxanne too sitting out, waiting to watch the smugglers at action? There was no movement down there, except a small form moving up the narrow beach. It was hard to pick out from this distance. It could have been a black dog meandering from boulder to boulder, perhaps Farrell's beast off its chain. It was soon lost from view under the cliff between Phonse's meadow and the water.

Closer at hand, she recognized Farrell stomping his solitary way past her house, heading for the bridge and his farm. Not a minute later, a dark figure with its hoodie up against the chill of the evening passed quietly by. She was thinking this must be a resident of the cottage closer to the bridge, when the air was suddenly split by the sound of motorcycles starting up and ripping off to town. How many? She could only guess. Surely more than one, but was it all three leaving—four if you counted Sid. She couldn't tell, the mountain's solid rock face caused such an echo to throb forth over the cove that the individual engines couldn't be identified.

But then there was nothing, which went on for a very long time. No sound, no movement at all across the community, except the scudding clouds across the moon. The sea remained calm with no boats leaving their tell-tale wakes. Just… nothing.

She sighed. It was a little boring, just watching the unevents of the evening. The dark was making her sleepy. And she really had to go to the bathroom, perhaps refresh her wine while she was up. Knowing her way around the house by now, she didn't bother with the lights as she went inside.

The wine had been left on the counter in her hurry to sit out and keep watch on the cove. As she poured a glass in the dim light of the moon, she again sensed the now familiar feeling of eyes upon her, as if she was being watched. The dancing lights through the back woods again caught her attention.

Carmel opened the screen door silently, watching the lights at play. Again, there seemed an urgency to their flickering.

"What are you trying to say?" she asked in a low voice into the windless night, feeling more than a little foolish in talking to the insects. Immediately, the woods behind the house sprang into life—a growl, a yelp, and a startled rustle—as something large crashed through the bushes and away from the house. The lights flickered out as if on a switch.

Another smaller rustle from the undergrowth nearby, and Hank stalked out into the silvered lawn, his tail fat with fury and his green eyes glinting in the moonlight.

"And what were you chasing?" she murmured. "Sorry to disturb you." Carmel bent and stroked his coat back into place, the handfuls of fur coming off in her palms evidence that he was missing Melba's daily grooming. He was probably hungry, she realized, and broke open an egg for him.

"I'll be round front if you want to join me," she advised the cat.

And finally things were happening in the cove. Carmel wrapped her quilt tighter around her shoulders as she watched a dark figure carefully picking its way down the lane towards the water. Wishing she'd thought to bring her binoculars with her, Carmel squinted into the landscape below. The light from the moon dusted a leather jacket. It must be Sid.

Another dark figure met him on the wharf and after a moment, the two climbed on board the boat. The low rumble of the engines reverberated through the cove in the cool night air. Lights on the mast blinked red and blue, while an incandescence lit the deck.

Remembering back to the stories of smuggling she'd read as a youngster, she wondered at the lights. Surely this activity was supposed to happen with a darkened boat, the light of the smugglers' moon enough to show their way?

This was rather thrilling, yet at the same time another part of her mind worried for Phonse. Had Bridget risen from her depressive mood enough to pass on her message? She hoped so, yet the men had still gone out on the water. Were the police watching, just as she was? She scanned the horizon, but there was only the one boat in the water. Even the ferry was tied up, having finished its runs at midnight. It was out of her hands, at any rate.

She was tired now, and the quiet of the night was lulling her mind. Only the desire to wait out the drama to its end kept her at her watchful post.

Chapter 11

But things were now stirring on the land side of the cove. Carmel's waiting ears caught a faint sound of crashing from the woods, almost a smashing, as if a large rock had tumbled down the gully, way back in the trees past Melba's house, up the mountain. Soon after that, from the corner of her eye, she caught the merest hint of a dark shadow slipping across the road to her right, heading down the gully she herself had climbed up that day not so long ago, when she'd found Peters' gutted body.

It must be Farrell's dog again. She shivered at the thought of that great beast on the loose. If that was what Hank had scared out of the woods, then her respect for the wild cat grew immensely. The shadow slipped away out of sight in an instant.

And then a car's headlights shone, coming up the North Point Road. A police car, the white of its body glowing in the moonlight. But it wasn't heading down the lane to Phonse's house and the wharf to wait at the ready to catch the smugglers red-handed. It slowly wound its way past the small gravel lane, past her house and down to the bridge where it finally stopped. Were they planning to go down by way of the gully to the wharf? That just didn't make sense. She craned her head over the veranda rails, the better to watch.

Four men climbed out of the car, one of them Darrow, she was almost sure.

And a minute later, more action! A media van, its lights off, pulled into her very own driveway. It bore the logo of Veronica's rival station, so it must be Smythe, setting off to on his farcical 'fairy hunt,' and using her yard as his access point. Totally pissed at this trespass, Carmel thrust on her canvas shoes, preparing herself to step down and tell him to clear off.

People poured out of the van—well, only two men poured out, but they made a lot of racket. The camera spotlight flashed on to—not Smythe—but a new face.

"This is Josh Landry with a news breaking story," he loudly whispered to the camera. Landry was a young man—very young. She recognized his face and name from various odd small stories he'd been allowed to present on the news—ones of rescued kittens and ducklings, and of unlawful graffiti—those that were beneath the attention-grabbing Smythe to relate. He looked very excited.

"I'm here on the scene at St. Jude Without," he continued in a low voice, thrilled to have this chance to be in the spotlight finally. "Earlier tonight, our head reporter Gerald Smythe headed out to this very spot, or at least close to it, to document his hunt for the rumoured fairies of this really weird cove. It started out as a light-hearted entertainment piece—yes—a bit of fun, because seriously, who believes in fairies in this day and age? With the police's continued inability to solve the puzzle of the recent bloody murder in this spooky community, rumours have been flying. Who killed Eric Peters? One suggestion that has cropped up on the website of *New Age Land* is the presence of vengeful other worldly spirits, who are determined to fight to keep their home safe.

"And yes, Gerald thought this was a bit of a lark," Josh Landry said, nodding sincerely into the camera. "He started out on this venture to make fun of the believers, and to disprove finally the presence of the fairies. Gerald wanted to do this all by himself, with no crew, in order not to scare away whatever might be out there. However, as his trusted Number 2 reporter, he wanted to keep me in the loop just in case anything happened.

"And something did happen." Josh leaned towards the camera. "Just minutes ago, I received a text from Gerald, alerting me that something was going wrong—very very wrong, on his expedition."

He reached into his pocket and held up his phone. "I'll read you what he said." A moment's pause as Landry flicked through screens and back-tracked, then a smile of satisfaction.

"'What the..' I mean, WTF, exclamation exclamation," Josh read from the small screen and smiled cheekily into the camera. He had learned well under Smythe's tutelage. "'Saw lights, all on cam, but attacked and bleeding an...'"

"If he'd had time, would he have added an 'arghhhh!' at the end of that text?" Josh asked in all seriousness. "There's been no contact since. So I'm here to find him, ladies and gentlemen, Josh Landry on his solo mission..."

The man behind the camera said something Carmel didn't catch.

"Well, yes, you're here too," Josh admitted. "It's up to us—a lone reporter and his cameraman—to find Gerald. Will he still be alive?"

The excitement was growing in his voice as he contemplated this.

"What, you phoned the police?" Josh exclaimed at another murmur from the crewman. "Well, I don't see them around. Yet another example...Yes, alright, already," he said, the irritation showing in his voice. "We'd better get a move on."

Josh Landry, ace reporter, turned to go up the path, the camera's light shining the way. "I'm sure he said it was up this way somewhere," he mumbled as he crashed off into the bushes. "He showed me a map."

All thoughts of going to bed were long gone now. Carmel knew she had to follow this through, although she decided to take the real path to the old graveyard which although was a further distance, was much easier going. Not that she was likely to lose the reporter, he was making far too much noise.

She waited at the entrance to the graveyard just as Josh broke through the trees.

"This then," he said into the mike, spreading his arm out around him. "This is where Gerald Smythe came in his search of the fairies of the cove. Is this where he was attacked and wounded, perhaps fatally?"

"Pan the ground," he told the camera man. "Let's look for blood."

The two conferred for a moment, the techie pointing to a trampled path.

"On we go," Josh said, back on camera. "I think I've picked up the trail."

He was walking backwards as he spoke, face towards the camera at all times, but tripped up over a fallen gravestone almost hidden in the tall grass. Lanky arms and legs flailing, he let out a small stifled scream, then caught himself as he realized he had tangled with an inanimate object only. "We can edit that out later," he said, dusting himself off. The two continued on their way, Josh watching more carefully now as he followed the trail. It led to the edge of the ravine.

"Holy cow!" Josh said as he spotted something. "Over here!" The cameraman rushed to join him. Carmel couldn't help herself. She ran too.

They all three looked down the ravine. There, over the edge, dangling by a blue nylon rope fastened securely on an ancient tree root, was Gerald Smythe. He did not sway in the wind, or struggle. His face was purple and his eyes were closed. He didn't move at all. Oops, he'd really done it this time.

"Oh my God, we found him!" Josh cried. He looked like he might wet his pants in excitement. "Is he dead? Are you getting the shot? Try climbing down for a better angle. Maybe you can get one of me discovering the body."

Strong lights instantly lit the scene from below, catching the cameraman in mid-scramble on the rocks and casting shadows upwards from the ravine. Josh's face became a parody of terror as the light caught his widened eyes.

"Who are you? What are you doing up there?" a voice thundered from below. A policeman roughly pushed past Josh, the officer climbing up the side of the ravine on his way to loosen Gerald's noose.

Radios crackled, lights shone and police were moving everywhere it seemed, all of a sudden. Carmel quietly melted into the background, loathe now to pass back into the dark graveyard by herself on this night of misdeed, but not wanting Darrow to find her in the company of Josh Landry. He might think she was a party to the young news reporter's antics.

Discretion won out. She made it back to her home with no incidents or unwanted sightings, just in time to see Phonse's boat pull back up to the wharf. She watched it warily, noting again the two figures climbing off and going their separate ways—Phonse to his home, and Sid (if it was him) coming up the lane. Had they played a part in what had happened to Smythe that night? She shivered to think of it, and couldn't for the life of her find a reason why they would do such a horrible thing or how they'd managed to do it. Smythe hadn't threatened to interfere with their activities, had he? The reporter was just a jerk, going about his self-promoting business, nothing to do with illegal importation of goods on the coast. Though she knew if he'd had a whiff of it, he and his camera would have been right on top of the story.

An ambulance rushed past, its siren unnecessarily warning other vehicles to get out of its way as it caught Carmel in its flashing red and blues. Lights came on, one by one, in all the houses scattered along the point, as the community was rudely awakened from its slumber.

Carmel surprised herself by waking up the next morning, having thought she'd never be able to fall asleep that night. She had lain for a long time, turning in her bed, processing all that had happened in that short span of time. First of all and most horrific—the image of Gerald Smythe hanging from the ravine should have been enough to prevent sleep from engulfing her. His darkened face and unmoving body with the noose obscuring his stupid bowtie swam vividly before her mind's eye. Practically in her back yard, as she had no need to remind herself, and that noise she'd heard—was it the sound of him being pushed off the meadow into the air below? Or had that happened earlier, before the men went out on their boat?

What was happening to this cove? she wondered blearily over the first coffee of the morning. First Peters' death, then Melba's poisoning—accidental or not—and now Smythe. Seriously thinking of giving up her lease on the house, refusing the offer to buy and just beginning her travels to get out of this place, she watched as Darrow's car pulled up into her driveway. What now?

She poured out a coffee for him as she topped up her own, and handed the cup to him as she greeted him at the door. He took it gratefully, and some colour returned to his gray face as he drank thirstily. He obviously hadn't had the luxury of a night's sleep after the goings on.

"Smythe?" she asked first thing.

"Alive," he said. "Thank God."

"He's not dead?" she said, surprised. "But he looked so..."

Darrow nodded. "Fortunately. He must have been hit over the head pretty hard, maybe with a rock. We haven't found it yet."

"But I thought..." she said. "He was hung, wasn't he? Or hanged. I saw the rope, and he was just dangling there not moving...."

"He's a lucky bastard," Darrow said. "His feet were just touching a rock ledge beneath him, enough to take his weight so his body didn't drag him down. And the bow tie, ridiculous as it was, saved his life. The noose couldn't tighten enough to choke him."

Carmel frowned in thought. "That's weird," she said. "A bow tie is just fabric, how did that stop the rope from cutting into his throat?"

"He wears a clip-on bowtie." Darrow smiled for the first time. "But don't tell anyone I told you that; it'll ruin his image. The clip was stiff enough to prevent any damage. Oh, he'll have a little bruising, but that's the least of his worries."

Carmel realized what this meant. "So he can tell you who did this to him?" she said with relief, although she wasn't sure she wanted to know.

"He's still unconscious," Darrow replied. "Whoever it was gave him a pretty hefty smack on the head. He's in ICU in the city."

"With Melba," Carmel said softly.

Darrow nodded. "Indeed."

She was raising her cup to her lips to drain the dregs of coffee when a thought struck her.

"He was filming," she said. "I heard Josh Landry, his fellow reporter say. Have you found his camera? That will give you some answers."

"We found the device he was using," said Darrow heavily. "He was using his phone for taking video, fitted out with a night vision app, we're told."

"They make such a thing?" Carmel asked, impressed, despite her interest in the story.

Darrow nodded.

"And?" she pressed him.

"We found it, as I said," he replied. "But it was smashed down the ravine. After the SIM card was deliberately removed. No sign of it anywhere."

"That's too bad," she said thoughtfully, pouring them each a fresh coffee. "You know, I was up last night."

"I saw you at the ravine," he said, no inflection in his voice. "I assumed you were helping Landry find Smythe."

"No, no," she replied hurriedly. "I was just following him and his camera guy. I mean, I was up on the veranda most of the evening."

He lifted one eyebrow but said nothing.

"How did you get there so fast?" she asked. "I overheard the camera guy say he'd phoned the police, but I saw you drive by before Josh got there."

"We were in the area," he replied. She didn't pursue it.

"Josh was talking, after he pulled up outside my house," she said. "He mentioned that Smythe got some footage of something. I don't suppose Josh took the SIM card for his own story?"

"Not possible," Darrow replied decisively. "He didn't make it down to the phone in time." He thought a bit more. "I'll need you to go through everything you saw and heard last night, in chronological order. That will help a bit," he said. "We have some missing pieces to this puzzle, and things are not making a lot of sense."

He took out a notepad, flipped it open and sat waiting expectantly, pen in hand.

Carmel told him almost everything about her sojourn on the veranda the night before—about seeing the lights outside, and even about Phonse and his companion (possibly Sid) going out on the boat and when they returned. She couldn't, however, bring herself to mention her suspicions about the smuggling (nothing was proven anyway), so to explain why she was out there at that late hour, she simply said she couldn't sleep.

"Hmmm," he said noncommittally after she'd finished, rereading his notes. "The cat."

She waited, and he looked up.

"Do you think it might have been Smythe he was attacking, not the dog?"

She shrugged. "I didn't see anything in the dark," she said. "Whatever it was, it was large enough to make a lot of noise when it ran."

She thought some more. "Didn't sound like a man yelping," she said. "But it didn't sound like Farrell's dog either." And she knew how deep that beast's growl was, having experienced it as it had pinned her to the ground the other day.

"Smythe has some deep claw marks on his face and chest," he said.

They both heard the noise at the window and looked up. It was Hank the cat himself, as if he knew they were talking about him. The large feline gave a pitifully small mew.

"Look at the size of that one," Darrow whistled. Then he winced. "The marks are consistent with a large cat leaping directly onto Smythe's face and clawing his way down the torso. That cat's not rabid, is it?"

No, she quickly assured him. Hank was quite healthy, to her knowledge.

"What would have made him go after Smythe like that then?" Darrow wondered. "That's unusual behaviour. A cat would normally stay hidden in the dark, unless the man was going after something it wanted to protect."

"I can't imagine," Carmel replied. "He's always been friendly with me. Maybe he's watched him on the news before, and found him as irritating as I do."

She said the last with such a straight face that Darrow was caught off guard. He gave her a look of surprise then, realizing she was joking, crinkled his warm brown eyes in a smile. Their eyes lingered together, for a fraction of a second.

"Tell me," she started impulsively, then bit her lip. She could hear faint whispers of Sister Mary scolding her against being a nosy-parker, even after all those years.

He raised his eyebrows in question, a smile on his lips.

Oh, what the hell, she thought. "I'm curious," she confessed. "How did a police officer from the Orkney Islands off Scotland, end up here?" She really did want to know.

"Not much of a story," he told her. "I'd visited here teaching a Criminal Studies course at the university— on smuggling it was—and liked the place. Not too far from home you realize."

She stopped to think, figuring out the distances. He was right, Scotland was relatively close, at any rate closer than the other side of her own country. She nodded.

"So there'd been some investigations into smuggling operations, not as big as Ireland's Eye of course, but I got involved, and, well, being ready for a change, I just never left," he told her.

Ireland's Eye had been a huge drug bust in the eighties, operating out of a tiny island off the coast. It had illustrated how difficult it was to police the thousands of kilometers of coastline of this larger island in the ocean.

"My wife seemed to like it here, at least, she said she did," he said, now looking off into the distance. "Of course, that changed."

Carmel automatically glanced down at his hand. Ring-free, she noted. That meant the wife was out of the picture, gone back to her homeland probably. Did that explain the sadness she saw in his eyes sometimes?

She and Darrow, both alone in their solitude. Everyone had baggage by the time they reached their stages of life. She almost reached out and touched his arm, but he moved toward the door.

Darrow took his leave shortly after that, but, of course, Carmel was soon joined by others as soon as the police inspector's car had pulled away. Bridget and she discussed the happenings of the night before over an impromptu lunch of salad and leftover chicken. Even Mrs. Ryan, seeing that Bridget was at Carmel's, lowered herself to drop in her back door in time for the sweets. She was not going to be left out of this gossip.

"He's not dead then?" Bridget asked, her eyes darkened. "That's a relief. There's been too much stuff happening here. But who could have done such a thing?"

"We're not used to such goings-on around here," Vee agreed. "But I won't say he doesn't deserve all he got, coming round poking his nose in where he's got no business to."

"That's a bit harsh, Vee," Carmel said. "Sure he's a pain, but no one should be almost murdered for being nosy."

Vee sniffed. "And who they going to try to blame for this one? Seems to me all this started when strangers started moving into the cove."

Carmel looked at her in disbelief. After the woman's previous treatment of her, she was ripe to interpret Vee Ryan's words in the worst way possible. But this took the cake—was she accusing her?

"You're not saying I had anything to do with all this?" she said in a joking manner, to cover the offense she'd taken at the woman's words.

Vee popped the last cookie into her mouth and swallowed her tea. "Nice biscuits for them as can afford 'em," she said sourly. "We don't live as fancy here in the cove as some do."

"Seriously, Mrs. Ryan," Carmel said, unwilling to let this go. It was unfair, what the woman had said, and she had no right to go around making loose accusations. "Do you really think that it was me who did these things?"

The older woman looked away uncomfortably. "I'm not saying nothing of the sort, of course," she said. "Just it's an odd coincidence, you turning up here right when Peters dies. You make friends with Melba, and there she is poisoned from her own garden."

"I'm sure no one poisoned Melba," Carmel said. "She's not right in the head. She made a mistake with the leaves. Mallow and monkshood do look alike."

Vee lifted her head and locked eyes with Carmel now. "I allow that's one mistake old Melba would never make," she said, venom dripping from her words. "That woman been making remedies since she was a kid. It's in her blood. There's no way she could have picked the wrong leaves, no matter if she is a little off in the head, and I'm not saying she is."

Bridget was looking at the pair with perplexity. She stood up, placing her hand on Vee's shoulder as she did so. "Let's go on now, Auntie Vee," she said

Mrs. Ryan stood, but was not yet finished.

"And you were seen, coming in from out back, last night," she hissed. "You could easily have taken that little snot Smythe out with a rock, creeping up on him."

Carmel's face was now red with fury. She stood up, about to order the older woman from her home, but Bridget already had her in hand and was dragging her out the door.

She let out a big sigh to decrease the tension in her shoulders after the pair left.

"Well," said a voice behind her, making her start. Roxanne stood on the threshold from the hallway, having let herself in through the front door. "How about that Vee?"

"What do you think of her nerve, coming in to my home and making those accusations?" Carmel sank back down to the table.

"I'm sure no one else believes that. Her credibility has been scuppered thanks to Smythe," Roxanne reminded her, a small smile playing at her lips. "Now, have another cup of tea."

Carmel poured up tea for two.

"What were you saying about Josh?" Roxanne asked. "About what Smythe had seen, I mean."

"He said Smythe sent him a text, I guess it must have been before he was hit on the head," Carmel said. "Said he saw lights or something." She laughed. "It was probably just the fireflies he saw," she continued, remembering back to the flickering lights of last night.

"I saw them too. They disappeared after the cat attacked Smythe."

Roxanne sat silently at the table, obviously lost in thought.

"Old Hank must have spooked him a lot," Carmel continued with a grin.

"You saw them?" Roxanne asked pointedly, cutting across her next words. "The lights?"

"Yeah, they're always there. Fireflies, but it's a bit late in the season for them. At least, I guess it is. I didn't think we had fireflies here. You know, like skunks and snakes, I thought they'd never made it over the straits to the island."

"I don't understand," Roxanne said. Carmel realized she was watching her with a perplexed look on her face. "I just... You?"

"What do you mean 'me'?" Carmel asked. But Roxanne was already headed out the door, calling good-bye.

"I should just put a revolving door on the back porch," Carmel muttered under her breath as she heard the squeak of the back screen door opening, and dragged herself back downstairs.

Phonse was sitting at the table now. "The tea's gone cold," he informed her.

"So put the kettle on," she sighed and turned to do it herself. She was still fuming from his mother's accusations and not feeling kindly disposed to him. Yes. It was probably what the psychologists would call transference, but that didn't make it any easier.

"Your mother," she found herself saying, unable to hold it in. "Your mother practically accused me of causing all this."

"All what?" Phonse asked, digging into the cookie tin, a frown on his face when his hand came up empty.

"This! The chaos! All the bad things happening around here." Carmel slammed the kettle down after freshening the pot. Drops of boiling water bounced on her arm, and she winced. Just another pain she could chalk up to Vee.

His open face fell, the childlike eyes now filled with concern. "No, she wouldn't have done that," he said, a touch of uncertainty present in his voice. "She likes you?" he added, unable to stop the question mark framing the ludicrousness of his words.

She wondered how he could ever have come from that woman. The one so happy-go-lucky, the other so sour. Carmel levelled her gaze at him, and knew she had to hold back. It wasn't his fault he had this mother. Mind you, he was not without imperfections and could certainly stand to grow up a bit, but that could stem back to his mother, too. The woman did everything for him, keeping him as a permanent boy.

But on the other hand, he allowed it to be so.

"Quite the goings-on last night," she said, trying to calm herself down.

His face brightened. "Yeah, what was on the go?" he asked. "Me and Sid were just coming back, and saw the ambulance up at Melba's. I thought she was still in hospital."

She told him everything she'd seen.

"Really?" He gave a long whistle. "Smythe is a bit of a dork, but hanged? Geez, that's not right."

"You know, Phonse." She had to bring it up. "You know the police were in the area. I think they may have been watching out for you, and whatever you were up to last night on the boat. And," she continued, holding up a hand to stop his interruption. "And I don't want to know whatever it is you were doing. Just wanted to warn you, that's all." Because obviously Bridget hadn't, being sunk in her own misery cloud as she'd been.

He laughed. "No, don't you worry about that," he said. "Sid had business up in Bauline, and it's faster to take the boat up than to go all that way around the mountain by car." He paused as her words sunk in. "What? You thought we were smuggling or something?"

"It had occurred to me," she said. And to others in the community too, she didn't add.

He paused, the smile gone from his face.

"Well, I'm glad they were watching," he said, all seriousness now. "Because now they can scratch me off their list. There's no way I could have been out on that boat and still done that to Smythe. And the person who strung up Smythe is the person who killed Peters, I can guarantee you that."

She nodded slowly. "That's what I've been thinking too," she said.

"There's just one thing," Phonse said, a frown creasing his brow. "My gear. It's usually kept on the boat, but when we got back to the wharf, I found it lying over the rocks, half in the water."

"Gear? Like nets and things?" she asked.

"No, my oilskin," he said. "My black rain coat that I keep on board. I can't figure out how it got from the cabin onto the beach."

"Is this something you should tell Darrow?"

"Maybe," he replied. "But I don't want to be bothering him if it turns out to be nothing."

"Maybe it was the fairies?" Carmel asked joking, harking back to her conversation with Roxanne. "They like to play tricks."

"True, they like to have their mischief," he answered with a poker face. "But they don't like the ocean. They won't go near the salt water."

She wasn't sure if he was carrying on with her or not, and raised an eyebrow in inquiry. He sighed, looking very uncomfortable.

"Look, it doesn't matter if you don't believe in them," he told her. "Just don't make fun. Never make fun of the fairy."

She watched as he walked slowly down the lane, his attention on an intense conversation on his cell phone. Something he'd said had triggered an itch in her mind. His rain coat, that's it. Why was that important? Not it being found on the rocks, she knew, there was something else...

Chapter 12

It was dusk and the sun was setting somewhere out there behind the bank of fog which had settled on St. Jude Without like a soft blanket of cotton wool, darkening the little cove before its time. As it moved down and around the houses and trees, it dropped the temperature several degrees from the warm late summer weather they'd been enjoying, heralding the oncoming fall. And the dampness over everything was inescapable, even after lighting a log fire in the crumbling fireplace and shutting all the windows. The flame caught the logs only reluctantly, too weak as yet to fight the moisture in the wood and air.

The book of pirates had made its way back to her coffee table—Phonse's little joke—she had no doubt. Carmel briefly considered using the book for kindling, then realized the leather binding which made it waterproof would also make it hard to burn.

Waterproof. Phonse's oilskin, dripping inside the otherwise dry cabin of his boat the day she'd found Peters' body. That was the anomaly which had been nagging at the back of her mind for so long. How had it gotten wet, when Phonse himself had been home before the rain started? And then she knew. Should she phone Darrow to tell him this, or would he as usual be ten paces ahead of her and have already have solved that puzzle?

Just a quick cigarette outside in the back, she promised herself, the mug of coffee warming her hands. She would phone Darrow to let him know what she'd remembered, and then go back to what she hoped would be a roaring fire in the parlour. The oncoming darkness mixed with wisps of fog to lend an enchanted air to the backyard, the familiar trees like beckoning wraiths behind the fading Queen Anne's Lace. Again, tiny lights flickered past the bushes leading to the old grave yard, barely visible through the mist. It was that time of the evening—the *gloaming* the Scots called it— the point between day and night when you could believe in the supernatural.

Was that a human figure beyond the trees by the ancient stones, or was it a solitary angel come to life? Her scalp prickled as she watched what looked to be an upright hooded form dance slowly, so slowly, back and forth where the fairy circle was. Dear God, what was it? This would have scared her at the best of times, but this fog and darkness lent a mysterious air to everything once familiar, and the attempt on Smythe's life last night was foremost in her mind. The figure melted back to blend with the trees so subtly that she felt it must have been a figment of her overactive imagination. Maybe just a tree bending in a rogue breeze.

A stumbling sounded in the wilderness, a muted cry. Was it human or animal? Again tonight, the flickering lights disappeared in an instant. Like a sentinel, Hank the cat was instantly at her side, hissing into the deepening murk, all his fur standing on end. He quickly glanced up at her and back to where the sound had come from, then started on his way, creeping low to the ground. That decided her. If Hank the cat was going into the fray, then she was too. Sharp of tooth and claw, with lightning fast reflexes, he was a good consort to have by her side.

But she wasn't going to rely on just a cat. Other reinforcements were at hand, and she'd be foolish not to use everything within her grasp. Carmel grabbed the phone from her pocket and dialed Darrow to let him know strange things were again happening behind her house and about the raincoat. Yet this call went unanswered and straight through to his voice mail. Unwilling to alert the intruder (or whatever it was) to her presence, she didn't leave a message, but did dial 9-1-1 to have at the ready should she be attacked, and was rather proud of herself for having thought of it.

The two crept along the path, Carmel quietly pushing past the bushes growing over the little used route. Clutching her cell phone, she prayed that there would be a signal available if necessary, so close to the sharply rising mountain. When she reached the stone angel, she paused to assess. Nothing was moving, except for the tops of the tallest trees swaying in the wind. You'd think the heavy wet fog would weigh down the wind, prevent it from blowing, or that the wind would blow the fog away. But no, it was as if the fog were a solid force yet immaterial at the same time, enveloping everything.

She sensed more than saw the cat slink from her side, heading over to the far edge of the old fairy circle, and made to follow him, but with a cry and a hiss, he flushed out his quarry from behind a boulder. A small woodland creature—squirrel or rat or young rabbit—darted through the shadows of the grass and disappeared, with Hank in hot pursuit.

"Way to go, cat," Carmel said aloud, the relief from the tension causing her to laugh out loud and relax against the cold marble angel. "Glad to be of assistance."

She turned to go back down the path, when the statue by her side moved.

Carmel swung round to it, her cell phone flying off to one side as her hands opened in a long forgotten startle reflex, adrenaline once again racing as she prepared to do battle. The stone was as immobile as it ever was, but a second figure had materialized by its side.

"Oh, it's you, Roxanne," she said, almost collapsing with relief this time. "Don't do that, you gave me such a fright." She looked through the bushes, trying to pinpoint which direction the phone had been flung. "Help me look for my cell, would you? I dropped it here somewhere. What are you doing here, anyway?" she asked in curiosity as she got down on her hands and knees in the murky underbelly of the raspberry bushes. "It's a rotten night to be out traipsing in the graveyard." She saw the dim glow not two feet away, and reached out her hand. So close.

"You won't be needing that," Roxanne's clear English voice said quietly in her ear, and the shorter, yet sturdier woman grabbed Carmel's outstretched arm and twisted it up behind her back. Carmel gasped with the sudden pain, then the pressure was eased just to the point where the pain merely hinted. Any movement from herself and it would be full on again. Her assailant knew what she was about.

"Roxanne, what are you doing?" Carmel asked in bewilderment. The phone's glow continued, tantalizingly out of reach. She could only stare at it helplessly, gaze glued to the spot where the LED light was fading with its automatic timer. In no time, it seemed, the phone had disappeared into the deepening gloom. She cursed the energy-saving mode she'd put on the damn thing. Now she couldn't even see its black outlines in the dusk.

"Get up," Roxanne whispered, emphasizing her words with a jerk to Carmel's arm. "All the way."

Getting up to stand was a difficult thing to manage without causing more jolts of pain up her arm, but she managed it, a fine sweat breaking out all over her body despite the cool air. Meanwhile, Roxanne's busy hands were tying a rope around her wrists and draping it over her shoulder, its tension ensuring that Carmel couldn't move an inch unbidden. She found herself frantically and ridiculously wondering if it were the same blue nylon rope which had hung Smythe from the ledge, and the same used by Phonse on his boat, even though she knew that was the least of her worries at that moment.

"Against the angel," the Englishwoman directed, then finished the job of securing her to the stone statue. Carmel tried to rock back and forth a little as Roxanne bent to rummage in a bag at her feet, but the angel was immovable, its weight anchoring her to it.

"Roxanne, why?" Carmel gasped out before the other woman straightened up, a large butcher's knife in her hand. "No, please don't!"

Roxanne looked with surprise from Carmel to the knife. Then it dawned on her what the other woman meant.

"Really, Carmel," she said in a lightly scolding voice. "I wouldn't hurt you. And you don't think I'd shed your blood here, do you? In the center of the fairy ring, of all places?"

"They'd never forgive me for tainting their special spot with spilled blood," she continued. "And then where would I be?"

Yet she continued to hold the knife in a threatening manner even as her eyes looked sadly at the other woman.

"Why tonight of all nights?" Roxanne asked, almost tenderly. "They'd finally shown themselves to me. And then that bloody creature scared them off!" She looked towards the bushes and waved the large knife. "I wouldn't mind cutting *its* throat," she added in an eerily chatty manner. "But time enough for that. First things first."

Carmel wanted to scream, but felt paralyzed, as the knife rested almost casually at her neck and could easily slip with the smallest movement. The only sounds she could force out of her mouth were tiny, terrified moans, which were quickly swallowed up into the heavy mist. Who would hear her on this cold fog-filled night? There had been no evidence of Sid at his bar, no seventies rock music coming from the old church that evening. Sid's opening hours were a law unto themselves, and this was obviously one of his off nights. She doubted that her small fearful whimpers would carry far through the trees to the road. There was simply too much standing in the way, cushioning all sounds from this tiny, well-hidden graveyard.

The other woman reached back into the canvas bag slung over her shoulder to withdraw a small prescription bottle. Carmel recognized it as one of the dusty pill containers from Roxanne's bathroom, and wished she'd paid closer attention to the contents at the time.

"Now," Roxanne said as she drew herself up in a brusque and practical manner. "I need you to swallow these. All of them, to make sure it takes." Roxanne opened the container and, climbing up onto a fallen grave stone next to the angel, forced the bottle to Carmel's mouth. She placed a strong finger and thumb along the hinges of Carmel's jaw, forcing her to open her mouth despite her efforts to the contrary. "All of them, mind," she warned as she put the bottle between Carmel's lips and shook the contents into her mouth. Maybe a dozen tiny pills filled her mouth, but with her senses heightened by terror, it felt as though the world was there. A bitter taste filled her mouth, a chalky texture coated her tongue as the little pills started to dissolve even in the dryness of her mouth. The Englishwoman had not let go of the carving knife all this time, and it waved dangerously close to Carmel's nose. The heavy steel glinted in the low light of the falling dusk, brushing past Carmel's hair, and she could swear she heard the sound of shaved strands falling past her ear.

"There." Roxanne was satisfied. "Now this water can wash it down." She held an opened water bottle to Carmel's mouth for her to drink it down. "Chin chin!" The water filled her mouth, forcing her body to choose between swallowing or drowning. She tried, oh she tried, to pocket some of the tiny pills to the sides of her cheeks or to spit them out with the water that was pouring down her chin, but she was aware of her failure to stem the course of the contents down her throat.

But maybe it wasn't so bad. She felt her resolve weakening as her body gave up its fight a single muscle at a time, though her mind still panicked, desperately searching for a way out, to save herself from this mad woman that just that day she had counted as a friend. She had invited her to live in her house, for God's sake, to share their daily lives.

"Why, Roxanne?" She forced herself to form the words. "Why are you doing this to me?"

The Englishwoman stood aside, watching her body reactions carefully. "You know the reason, Carmel. Don't play dumb with me."

She could only stare uncomprehendingly at the other as she bent down closer to her.

"You're not buying my house," the other woman hissed in her face. "How could you even think of it?" Her breath was foul and stale, but Carmel hardly noticed it in her disbelief.

"House?" she managed to get out. It didn't make sense. Nothing here was making sense. The events of the past few days, the interminable lights, now this.

"Besides, you found me out," Roxanne continued with certainty. "Phonse's raincoat was the last straw. Right after he left your house this afternoon, the police were down at his wharf and picked it up. I knew I had to act fast, so I grabbed everything I'd need and hid out up here, waiting for you. There was no doubt that he'd told you about it, and you were immediately on the phone to your special friend the cop."

"What?"

"Oh, yes, we've all seen how close you two are," she said. "The whole cove has been watching."

"The raincoat..." Carmel's mind raced back to the afternoon. She remembered seeing Phonse on his phone as he was walking down the laneway. "No, that was Phonse who must have told Darrow... But what did his raincoat have to do with this?" Her voice was slurring as if drunk.

Roxanne cocked her head to one side. "I used the coat to prevent getting covered in Smythe's blood of course. It was a perfect fit—covered me from head to foot. It wasn't the first time, of course."

She remembered now the black figure she'd seen the night of Smythe's hanging, down by Phonse's wharf. Farrell's dog broken off its chain and out on the prowl, she'd thought at the time—yes, it had been a dangerous beast, but not the one she'd thought it was. But if Roxanne had done the deed to Smythe, then had she been the one to off Peters? Carmel's befuddled brain couldn't see it.

"Did you kill Peters?" she asked, forcing her lips to form the words. Carmel didn't know what it was that Roxanne had given her, but one dim part of her brain told her to keep her muscles moving as much as possible to work against the obvious sedating effects. And any reader of mysteries knew it was important to keep the villain talking in order to increase one's chances of survival. "Why?"

"The man was going to ruin everything," Roxanne said. She looked about her almost tenderly. "This sacred ground would have become a suburb for the rich, its topsoil raped and all its magic dissipated. Where would the fey go then? No, I had to save it for them. And they have rewarded me. They showed me their lights this evening. The end justifies the means."

Carmel could only stare at her with dawning horror. Fairies? Oh dear God, the woman was mad, her childhood obsession had spilled over the line to reality. Keep her talking.

"But how?" she forced out. "He was a big man, so much larger than you. How could you have flung him over the bridge?"

"Easy-peasy," Roxanne said with pride in her voice. "I was talking with him earlier and arranged to meet him down by the bridge. Men are led by their genitals, aren't they? I hid in the trees until he got there, then I stood on a boulder and slit his throat. Learned to do that in Sumatra, but not with a human of course."

Carmel shuddered to think of it.

"That's the first time I used Phonse's raincoat," Roxanne continued conversationally, happy to share her deeds with a captive audience. Carmel knew it was important to keep her talking, yet on the other hand, knew all hope of mercy had fled by being privy to the tale. Friend or not, Roxanne couldn't afford to let Carmel live now. "That heavy rain was perfect—it washed away all the blood by the time I got back to the boat."

And the puddles under the black rain coat on the boat were the clue she could have picked up on. If only she'd realized it sooner.

"The yellow glove," Carmel said, remembering. "Yours...?"

"Clumsy, I know," Roxanne said. "Losing that on the way. However, with all the garbage and detritus washed up by the ocean, I wasn't too worried about it standing out. Really, the people around here don't seem to care about litter; they're living in their own filth.

"It was easy enough to topple him over the bridge and into the gorge. Simple physics," she continued, lost in her happy reminiscences. She could have gone on but for the shrill interruption coming from the brush below. Carmel's phone. Its LED light shone through the murk. *So close*, she thought, willing Roxanne to look away for a moment. She could almost touch it with her foot. If she could just hit the receive button...

But the ringing tones broke Roxanne's train of thought and brought her back to the present.

"We'll leave that, shall we?" she said, kicking the lifeline out of reach, further into the tall grasses of the graveyard. The ringing continued once, twice, then was silent.

"Let's get you sorted then," Roxanne said as she placed the knife in her mouth to free her hands. She untied the nylon rope from the statue then neatly wrapped it round Carmel's other wrist, binding them both behind her back. Carmel stumbled a little, her body now relaxed and her balance off. She could feel the drug coursing through her blood. Although her mind told her to be afraid, her body was allowing the terror to seep out of her. But she fought to keep the connection alive. *Had that been Darrow returning her call? Where was he now? For that matter, where was Hank the cat?* she wondered blearily. *Why hadn't he attacked the woman at the first hint of danger?* Keep interacting, something deep within her said.

"Melba?" she slurred, as Roxanne began to lead her through the old graveyard.

"Mind your step," the other woman told her. "Yes, Melba," she continued, shaking her head. "I hated to do that. I know the fey consider her a friend. But she knew what I'd done to Peters. She told us that. I couldn't risk her blackmailing me later on. Even though she knew I'd done the whole cove a favor. She's an old woman; she really shouldn't have survived that tea I substituted for her mallow."

"She's strong, but I don't think she knew. She was just having us on... being important..." Carmel mumbled as she slowly made her way down the dark path. They were headed to Melba's house. What did Roxanne have in mind? Was she going to cut her throat and toss her over the bridge as she'd done to Peters?

The cell phone ringing sounded again behind them, faintly now. Carmel cast one last longing glance towards it, and thought she could see its glow. No, wait, it was up in the trees, there were many phones, dancing in an agitated frenzy. Her drug befuddled mind was confusing the fireflies with the phone. It was too late, she realized. The drugs had taken a strong hold on her system. She was even unable to feel the horror any longer. She just had to work at concentrating on keeping Roxanne talking.

"But Smythe..." Carmel was determined to keep her mind and body active in any way she could.

Roxanne laughed. "What an idiot; he really brought that on himself, didn't he?" She tugged on the rope, causing Carmel to stumble and fall. Oh, to sit, just to let her body lie down. She felt herself becoming heavy and soft, like an overstuffed armchair, immovable.

"Get up," Roxanne said sharply. Carmel felt a kick to her side, but it really didn't hurt. That spot was so far away, so far removed, there was no pain at all. Even the steel blade of the knife held at her throat had now warmed to her body heat. "We're not there yet."

Where was there? Carmel wondered hazily.

"I thought it a nice touch, hanging him off the side," Roxanne continued. "Couldn't shed blood on the fairy ground, of course, but off to the side? That's another one the world will be happy to see the end of."

"But..." Carmel's mouth felt numb. "He's not dead..."

Roxanne stopped in mid-stride, anger visibly washing over her face even in the near-dark. "Did you say he's not dead? How can that be?"

"His bowtie saved him..." she said, not entirely sure she was forming the words.

"Well, I'd better fix that, and no time to lose," Roxanne muttered, hurrying Carmel along the way. "Here we are."

She prodded Carmel in the back. "In you go," she told her brusquely. "By the time you're found you'll be long dead with that load of benzos in you. Even if you don't, no one will know to look for you here, and Melba's still in the hospital."

Benzodiazapines. The old pill bottles had held valium, the central nervous system depressant which was now coursing through her veins. No, Roxanne hadn't wanted to cause her pain, but was still ensuring her death leaving her here to die of an overdose or exposure.

They'd stopped in front of Melba's ancient root cellar, the solid wooden door now yawning open into a dark blacker than night. Damp air, colder than the surrounding fog, rose up out of its depths, smelling of earth and rot and old vegetables leftover from years of winter, perhaps a dead rodent or two. Bile rose in Carmel's gorge, and panic surged past, cutting through the overdose of sedatives coursing through her veins.

She couldn't go into that dark hole. The darby-boos lived there. Panic stricken memories of the tiny closet under the convent stairs swam up to her and threatened to drown what rational mind remained. Of course, it was Sister Mary Oliphant, that dreary, stern, bitter woman who had her charge that first year that Carmel's mother had deposited her with the nuns. The Sister who had later disappeared from the convent without a word of good-bye when her sins had been found out, but not before the damage had been done to Carmel's tender psyche. But this realization couldn't stop the full blown panic tide from engulfing her at the threat of the yawning maw of the pitch black root cellar. The five-year-old child inside her was terrified.

Her body stopped of its own accord, unmindful of the press of steel at her neck. She could not. She felt her stomach pitch and heave as its contents emptied, down the front of her shirt and onto the ground below. She barely felt the heat of the bile or the sting of the knife as it sliced her skin as she crumpled down, held up only by the pain in her arms stretched up and behind her. And even this pain was resolving itself, fast receding into the surrounding fog until it too became just another sensation dimly sensed from a far off land.

When she opened her eyes again, there was nothing to be seen. How much time had passed she didn't know, couldn't begin to estimate. Her hands were now free—Roxanne must have untied them when she was unconscious. The darkness was so intense and cold it bit into her bare skin, and it was a minute or two before she realized her whole body was shivering. Her mouth felt like sandpaper and grunge, but a sharp pain in her neck caused her to reach up. It was sticky, she realized, with blood, as was the whole front of her shirt. She dimly remembered having thrown up—how much was blood? Not wanting to probe the wound deeply for fear of re-opening it, she shifted carefully to her knees. The smell of earth and rot was overpowering. She must be in the root cellar itself. How high was it? She tentatively lifted her arm above to feel for the roof. There, she touched the old wood, surprisingly dry yet cold like everything else in this unfathomable world.

The pain in her side kicked in with the movement, and she quickly crumpled back into a fetal ball to ease it. If she only stayed in one spot, didn't move a muscle, she found that the earth became warm almost comforting, almost soothing. It must be the fairies calling her name in their tiny distant voices, calling her to join them in their dance. "Not yet," she mumbled to them. "Just another minute more. Let me sleep."

But they called and called insistently, not letting her settle, and ran over the turf above her head, their light feet dancing. Then she heard them scratch and mew at the old wooden door of the root cellar, demanding entrance.

Carmel lifted her head, the action clearing her thoughts a little and allowing memory to flood back in, a drop here, then a rivulet, and then the force of a mountain stream after a storm. She was cold and ached, and lying in Melba's root cellar.

And that was the cat at the door.

"Hank?" Her voice was barely more than a sandpaper whisper. She turned to the sound and dragged herself toward it. The splintery wooden door blocked her way and, leaning against it, she tried to push. But the sturdy Roxanne had shoved it solidly in place, the oak pole firmly holding it.

She heard more of the thundering sound, like a herd of caribou hooves echoing through the ground from a distance. "Over here!" a deep Scottish accent said, surprisingly close but muffled through the wood. Then with a creak and a shout, the barrier was gone and the early dawn broke over her, the sweet dew of the grass washing her face as she fell back into the sanity of her own world.

The ambulance ride and the subsequent stint at the hospital emergency department passed in a hangover-like haze, her mind conveniently forgetting the more unpleasant aspects such as the necessary but dignity-stripping stomach pumping to rid her body of the last of the drug. Not to worry, Phonse insisted on rehashing it all on the mercifully short drive home, having been by her side the whole time.

"Oh man, it was so gross," he said, long greying curls whipping round his face as he drove with one arm out the window of his truck, his eyes hidden by mirrored aviator shades. "I mean, you hear about these things, but to see it? There were tubes up your nose and in your mouth. I always thought for a stomach pump they'd place a vacuum sort of thing down your throat, you know?"

Carmel remained silent. Eyes closed, leaning against the head rest, she wished this ride would be over or that Phonse would at least shut up.

"Thank God, I saved your life," he continued blithely unaware of her thoughts. "If I hadn't phoned Darrow about the raincoat, he'd have never been in the cove."

"I was the one who told you to do that," she reminded him, but her voice was so scratchy she could barely pick out her own words. She didn't have the strength to point out to him that it was the cops picking up the raincoat that had alerted Roxanne and caused her to take action.

"What's that?" he asked but didn't pause for an answer. "Yeah, who'd have thunk little Roxanne was the one behind all this? She seemed so quiet and nice.

I'd never had rented her the house if I'd known she was crazy, you know."

He pulled up into her driveway as he said these last words. Bridget was waiting on the veranda.

"Help me bring her upstairs," Bridget directed her cousin as she opened the door of the truck. That being accomplished, Phonse was banished from the house, his excited chattering not missing a beat.

"Hope you don't mind," Bridget said, one eyebrow raised. "You look like you could use some quiet. Now, drink this tea down.

"Just orange pekoe," she said, noting the look of alarm on Carmel's face. "Not mallow or anything else horrible. Good for what ails you, in any circumstances."

Her bed was soft and warm, and she spent the day drowsing in her nest. Bridget must have been looking in on her, for at one point she found a fresh cup of tea along with hot scones oozing butter. She'd set up the TV, too, perhaps in case she got lonely, with the international news on, running through the daily horrors of the world. The sound was muted so as not to disturb her sleep.

Carmel idly watched the streaming commentary at the bottom of the screen as she sipped her tea. Not that there was much cheerful happening, with hurricanes and wars and bombings, and not that she was really taking it in. But through her grogginess, the word Ukraine caught her eye and she sat up just a little. Ruscan's homeland. The Russians were trying their best to annex it but the Ukrainians were fighting back. Men in fatigues conferred outside a large stone building, hard to tell which side they were on, but there, in the back, was a head of brown curls. The man turned towards the camera and she caught the familiar profile, just a glance, before the hurricane in the Philippines demanded the viewer's attention.

Was it...? Could it have been Ruscan, alive and home? She sank back into her pillow, not sure now that she had not dreamed it.

When next Carmel opened her eyes, it was to see Darrow seated next to her bed, his gaze focused out the window at the sun setting on the water. The day had warmed up and dispersed the fog, returning the late summer weather to all its glory. The red and golden sky outside reflected on his face, softening the crags born of a lifetime working for the side of justice. Carmel examined the Inspector more closely. Despite the crooked nose, and the slightly uneven height of his eyebrows that lent his face a slightly squished appearance, his was an attractive face when it became familiar. *It grew on you*, Carmel thought. And his eyes were kind.

Those same brown eyes turned to focus on the woman in the bed. The warmth therein softened the cragginess of his face and she felt a glow of comfort and contentment fill her.

"All right, then?" he asked softly.

She nodded. Her head was now clearer than it had been at any time in the past twenty-four hours.

"Thanks," she said, simply.

"It was the raincoat that did it," he said, unconsciously echoing Roxanne's words of the previous evening. "As soon as Phonse told us, it all clicked into place."

Carmel started up as the implications of his words dawned. "As soon as?" she said, her voice finding new strength. "He told you in the afternoon. Why did you wait so long? She could have had me dead." She flopped back on the pillows, her energy spent by this small outburst.

"We had no proof," he said. "We were watching her house. Unfortunately, she'd already left, must have been hiding out in the grave yard, waiting to lure you out."

"What made you go up there?" she asked. "Did you know what she'd done?"

"Not at the time, no. But I'd seen you had called, and then you weren't answering your phone." He paused then and stood, walking the short distance to the other small window in her loft bedroom. "When my team alerted me that Roxanne had returned to her house, so late at night, we realized she may have been off creating more mayhem. Your car was still there, but you weren't answering your phone or your door. Yet your lights were on at that late hour and the coals of a fire were burning in the grate. I knew you wouldn't have left that."

She remembered guiltily that, yes, she had forgotten all about lighting the logs. Anything could have happened while she'd stepped off into the graveyard. She could have burned the house down, not keeping an eye on the flames. Still, she hadn't meant to be long. Certainly had not intended to be abducted and drugged, she comforted herself.

"I thought I'd ask the kids if they'd seen you," he continued, unaware of the conversation ongoing in her head. "But by the time I'd reached the graveyard, they were gone."

"There weren't any kids around last night." She frowned, remembering the perfect silence of the fog shrouded night.

"I saw their flashlights round the back of your house," he informed her.

"You mean the fireflies," she said with a smile. "I was confused when I first saw them too."

He turned and looked at her, a strange expression on his face. "No, it must have been children playing," he stated authoritatively. "I can't think what else would be making the light. There are no Lampyridae—or fireflies—on this island."

Carmel was quiet for a moment as she thought about what his words signified. Something had been making the dancing lights out back, but she shoved that aside for the moment, for to think about this might make her as crazy as the Englishwoman.

"As I said," Darrow continued firmly. "The children were gone. I tried phoning you again. It was then I found your cell in the grass, and the signs of the grass trampled down under foot. You can thank the cat," he added. "It showed us the root cellar. We'd been about to bring in the dogs."

Hank, appearing as always when being the topic of discussion, jumped up on the bed and mewed his funny little noise. She scratched under his chin and bent to bestow a kiss on his wide black head.

"We couldn't have that now, could we?" she said to him as she cuddled him into her arm. "Dogs, indeed? And you saved my life."

She smiled up at Darrow, who was shaking his head.

"You weren't near death," he assured her. "You'd appeared to have vomited up most of the pills. And they were years out of date. I'm surprised the benzodiazepine had so much effect on you."

This reminder of the undignified circumstances he'd found her in caused her to turn her head away. It had been a horrible ordeal, and he was making it sound like she had over-dramatized the whole thing. "I have a sensitive system," she replied as huffily as she could. "I nearly died."

After a long pause, Darrow cleared his throat. "Well, then, you're settled. I'll be off. Be seeing you," he added.

She quickly turned back to face him, only to see him leaving.

"When?" she called out to his departing back. He stopped short and spun on his heel. "When will I see you?" she asked again, registering that her voice was taking on a slightly querulous tone.

He paused at the doorway.

"That depends," he said, a smile breaking over his face like an ocean wave on the granite beach. "When do you set off on your travels?"

Carmel took her time considering the answer to this question. With all that had happened in such a short span, one part of her wanted to shrug off this strange little cove and embrace the relative civility of such islands as, say, Sicily with its Mafioso, or Alcatraz, or even Hainan, the ancient Chinese island of imprisonment.

Yet. And yet. This was still her perfect base—a small rural community, yet close to the city and its airport. She still had the option to buy, and would not likely find a cheaper bargain with such proximity to the ocean. True, Roxanne was no longer an option to share with, but the right low rental would certainly attract a university student with a car to live with her. And Bridget, that warm-hearted, temperamental hippy chick was here, even Phonse, the attractive Peter Pan. She wanted to stay, or at least keep the house as a home base.

There was also the added mystery of the fairies. If such things existed, then they surely lived in her backyard, and she found herself hungering to learn more about this phenomenon.

And there was Darrow, the upright Scot. Yes, a lot of reasons to keep her round.

"I'm not going anywhere just yet," she said softly. She was looking only at Darrow, yet she caught the slight movement in the darkest corner of the room, the barest whisper of a feathered hat nodding.

THE END

ABOUT THE AUTHOR

Author Liz Graham lives in Newfoundland, a large, mysterious wild place in the North Atlantic which is full of history and myth and weather and water. She is the author of the Carmel McAlistair mystery series of which *The Cut Throat* is the first. Her second book *The Garrote* will be out soon. Both books are available in paperback and e-book.

Liz is presently renovating her '20's bungalow in historic St. John's, which is also an Air B & B in the summer months. It's a great way for Liz to meet people and welcome visitors to this island.

Visit Liz at her website: www.LizGraham-Author.com.

Made in the USA
Charleston, SC
27 February 2017